SUNLIGHT

TITANS, CRANES & MONSTERS GAMES

KRISTIAN JOSEPH

Northern Luck
Publishing © 2020

For Veronica, Stanley, Sheila & Kelvin

1

FIREWORKS

At the southern heart of Kingdom Isle was a capital city booming and full of life known as Sovereign. Six hundred square miles of streets paved with gold boasted buildings as high as the sky, and others more than a thousand years old. It was a financier's dream, a hustling, bustling city of vibrant life forever outgrowing its limits, where anyone could make something of themselves. Tonight, it was alive with celebration, and at its central point hundreds gathered, those who had been lucky enough to get tickets for the Old Abbey Gardens on New Year's Eve. Under black and starry skies, the Abbey's limestone glowed with the lights of theme park adventure. Ferris wheels, teacups, cotton candy, beers and bellows of laughter.

Above the fair, an open field and grass verge overlooked the celebrations. Here, families and friends sat and cherished the moment with one another, making memories to last a lifetime. Lost in the moment among them lay two teenagers in love; with smiles shining bright they looked to a sky full of promise. The young man's hair was blond and slicked back, buzzed at the sides. Standing, he was tall, and in brighter light had light blue eyes. His full name if you were to ask him was Samuel James Royle, but to anyone special he was Sam. Often quiet, he lay now with his arm around his young love, wishing this moment would never end. Snug under his arm lay Hope Farrow. She had light brown hair and hazel eyes, and she felt she could lie there forever if either of them had the choice.

"Sam, did you hear me?" asked Hope, well aware he wasn't listening.

"No, sorry – no. I'm looking at the stars," said Sam, locked in a gaze, knowing what tomorrow would bring and that he couldn't do a damned thing about it. The news was most unexpected, and he wanted to cherish this moment forever.

"The stars will be there every night." Hope sat up and took in the view again: a thousand different fairground lights and rides. It wasn't often anyone got to see inside the Abbey Garden walls. Only a select few ever won the people's lottery and only the exceptional won at this time of year.

"Well, what were you going to say?" asked Sam. He sat up and looked into eyes that shone like on the first day they met. Even on that cold rainy day when they were six years old, they had kept him warm despite the exchange of bad news under a stranger's umbrella. Hope was the only one who was ever there for him, the only one.

"I got in," she said, breaking his reverie.

"Got in where?"

"Got into school, silly, I'm going to be a nurse! If you take your engineering scholarship at St Peter's, we can still get to each other in an hour or two tops," Hope exclaimed with a smile on her face, too joyous to slow down; but when she looked at Sam, he didn't share her reaction. "What's wrong? I thought you would be happy."

"You know I am, I'm so proud of you," he replied, as kind and calm as ever.

"Well, you don't seem like it, you don't seem yourself."

Hope was right, Sam had been acting strange all night: he was looking at everything as if it was the last time he would ever see it: the sky, the Abbey, the rides, and most of all, her. Sam looked down and slicked back his hair as if there was something he needed to say but he didn't want to take anything away from the moment.

"I'm not going to St Peter's."

"I don't understand … I thought –"

"I've been drafted for service," he said in disbelief at his own words, even though hearing it aloud made it all the more real. Sam pulled the letter from the top pocket of his khaki jacket and Hope took it from him, scrambling across each line in the hope that it wasn't true. She held back tears as denial took hold.

"This can't be right, you have a scholarship, how can they? The Far East and Great States are at war; what if we're next, what if –"

Sam knew that he couldn't do a damned thing about it. The only brothers he had ever known had been in the Kingdom military academy with him from the age of six. After the death of his parents, the state had raised him; his training was a debt to be repaid with study or combat, and bad luck had drawn the latter. He would lead his platoon, his brothers, and he couldn't have it any other way.

"We won't go to war, the Kingdom will last, no matter how bad it is abroad."

"What if you don't come back?"

Sam leant in close, put a hand to her cheek and, hiding his fears, whispered the words, "I'll always come back, but I need you to promise me something."

"If you tell me what it is, then I might," she replied, hiding her emotions, although not as well as he.

Sam sat with an odd quiet about him, considering it was the eve of his deployment. He wasn't too bitter at the news of two more years of service, his never-ending re-enrolment, even if it brought a temporary end to his progress in the field of engineering. He had to do what was expected of him, for they put a roof over his head, gave him an education, and another family after the one he had lost.

"Don't worry about me, I'll be fine. Worry about your studies, your career."

"Sam, not a day goes by when I don't worry about you."

"Then can we at least live tonight as if tomorrow will never come? All I want to do is take my mind off it."

Hope paused. "Of course we can."

She got to her feet to explore the funfair and Sam

looked up to see her surrounded by fairground lights and a blissful night sky, and it was everything he had ever wanted. It was at that moment that he took to one knee as if to stand, but foolishly stayed there. Hope went to turn around, having not noticed, but he took her hand and she turned to see something she never expected.

"Sam, what are you doing?" she said, gasping, and covering her nose and mouth with her hands. Part of her wanted to hit him, part of her wanted to kiss him, laugh and cry.

"Will you marry me?" At this question Hope did something just as spontaneous. She tackled him, flattening him on the ground, and they tumbled and rolled together. She ended up on top and couldn't help but smile in triumph.

Sam laughed; he felt like an idiot. "If I was in the field, I'd be dead right now."

"Aye, Lieutenant, this is what you get for being so foolish as to try and marry me." Hope tried to keep herself from laughing; she pushed her hair back and continued, "I can't believe you; did you even think this over? Do you even have a ring?"

"Yes – well, no. Not yet. I didn't have time."

"Didn't have time? You had time to think this was a good idea, but no time to, time to – sometimes I wonder how I fell for you, my mother warned me, you know …"

"You still haven't answered!"

Hope looked at the fool she had fallen for. He was strong, but kind, and it was so hard to tell what he was thinking. Despite how stupid he could be, he was clever most of the time, and though she tried to fight it, she had the sudden urge to kiss him. They closed their eyes and forgot everything around them.

"So, what'll it be?" asked Sam.

"Ask me again when you come home."

"I will."

"Promise?"

"Promise."

They sat, up and held each other's hands before turning to see the golden fair, filled with a thousand lights. It took Sam a few moments to realise that he had got the answer he wanted; it would have been foolish for her to say yes and then spend all that time waiting. People seemed to stay engaged forever, and married, too – he would at least get one more chance to do it all over again, and this time he would have a ring, this time he would do it right.

The pair finally got to their feet and waltzed hand in hand through the crowds to watch the juggling jesters and clowns on stilts do tricks. The sweet smell of fresh donuts and fried chicken filled the air, but all Sam had was state-sponsored coupons, and, sadly, not enough of them. Still he walked with his chin held high alongside his love, passing stall after stall of freshly baked brownies and carnival games. It wouldn't be long now until the fireworks, until the New Year. The crowd was thick and too much for two lost souls without any money, so they turned a corner between two stalls to get away.

In the back alleys, the lights faded, the sounds of

celebration became but a mumble, and two parliamentary honour guards stood ahead, dressed in black with the gold Sovereign crown wrapped in thorns printed upon their armour. They leant on a metal fence that stretched all the way around the Old Abbey. When Sam saw them, he froze. The hairs on the back of his neck rose as he felt only cold and struggled to see. It was happening again, the fear, the feeling. Sam had a vision, and in that vision, he saw the guard on the left wearing white and standing deep underground within concrete walls. The one on the right was dead and buried. Behind them smoke billowed from the Abbey, and when it began to settle, the fences were much higher, and all the windows were dark and shattered.

"You there, step back," said the one on the left, but the only thing that could pull Sam away was Hope's warm, reassuring hand. He breathed again and came to, unaware of his surroundings for a moment until the barrel of a gun raised high caught his eye. Sam raised his hands, as did Hope, and they stepped back as instructed.

"Are you deaf? Go back to where you came from, keep movin' or we're takin' you in," said the guard on the right. He was shaking, beyond nervous, for the growing unrest within the city made everyone a threat.

"Wait, he's an ultra," Hope said on instinct, and although Sam would never have wanted her to state his position in public, he nodded. He tried to ignore his vision and play a game, for the man on the right wasn't dead yet. The honour guard put down his rifle and moved forward, forced his hand into Sam's pocket, and snatched his papers. After a bitter squint at them, the guard stuffed them back in Sam's pocket before stepping away to salute a man much younger than himself.

"At ease," said Sam, knowing that it was rare for either of them to see an ultra in the flesh. An ultra wasn't an honour guard's business: they were no one's business but their own. Still, many knew of the Kingdom legends about ultras: raised by the state from such a young age, born to fight, born to lead, born to kill.

"We're ever so sorry, you took a wrong turn, sir; the fair is back there!"

Sam turned, stumbled, and took Hope by the arm, and they marched back toward the party after their harsh reminded of tomorrow. Sam was pale; he hid his panic behind futile coping mechanisms. They walked back through crowds now thick and busy again.

"It happened again, didn't it, Sam," Hope said, but he ignored her and kept trying to walk. "*Sam.*"

"Yes," he said, before turning to her with a look of great concern. He knew that his problem couldn't be solved, and that it pained her. Hope had become a nurse to help people, but she couldn't help the one who meant the most. She put on a brave face, took him by the arm, and walked him back out towards the large iron gates from where they came. They passed the Ferris wheel and headed down the hedgerow-bordered path, back out into a more open space. Sam could breathe again; now he had the space to think and realise that his thoughts weren't real, as Hope hugged him tight and placed her head upon his chest.

"Someday we'll find someone who can help you."

No one can help me, Sam thought to himself, before saying the words, "I hope so." He cracked a smile in fear of ruining the evening, but as he looked back into the eyes of his love, he knew nothing could. They held each other close and he realised that tomorrow he would be gone at four in the morning. He wanted to run, to go anywhere with her, but there was nowhere to go.

"Have you ever seen anything … you know … anything about me in your visions?" asked Hope, interrupting his trail of thought.

"No." Sam chuckled; that was the truth. His visions were wild and free, of all colours, a red sun, a stone man, images of freedom and flight, of great machines and struggle. They were endless and involved many people around him, but never Hope.

"Can we at least stay for the fireworks?"

"I wouldn't miss them for the world."

2

BETTER DAYS

A stone's throw from the Old Abbey, down the cobbled backstreets of Bakersville, was a quaint family restaurant with the finest wine and seafood in the whole city. It had passed down through the Frist family from generation to generation. The first Frist hailed from the Union state of Reach, across the dark and stormy Channel. A proud fisherman with a passion for cooking, he worked hard with his hands and his meals were for a time of plenty. When the great Union famine struck his nation, every catch was counted, every spoil confiscated, and in their place came dry rations.

Mister Frist was not a man willing to fight, but he had looked out to the sea and dared to dream. Upon breaking point, when the soldiers changed their shifts, he had taken his rowing boat and sailed into the dark, unforgiving Channel. Upon stormy seas with ten-foot waves, he cursed the sea and prayed. Somehow his prayers were answered, for Frist made it to the southern coast and onto Sovereign. For years he cleaned and washed glasses at an inn to make a living, saving the little he could. Then everything changed: he overheard the owner, a troubled and bankrupt financier, drowning his sorrows at the bar, commanding everyone to drink the whole place dry. Frist made his move and bought the deed, and soon after the traditional delicacies and culture of Reach became increasingly popular.

Sovereign became Frist's home, a liberal place, the last testament to democracy left on earth, where a street cleaner could work hard and with some good fortune become the owner of a successful business. The restaurant was very much the same then as it was now, except Frist was gone and another had taken his place. It was still the same old collection of small, dark candle-lit rooms, rich red and part stone, accessorised with wooden furniture. The pastry-based desserts were famous and the only way to get a table was to put down a name months in advance.

Late in the evening on New Year's Eve, two couples had planned to meet and celebrate together. Already sitting at the table awaiting their company in a candle-lit alcove was Nathan Sahl. Nathan was in military service dress of navy blue with gold trim. Nathan was tall with a strong physique, neck and jawline. He had dark brown hair, short at the sides, with a streak of silver, and his wide brown eyes were lost as he sat across from his love. He couldn't help but laugh, he could not help but smile. Across from him was his young wife Rose. Rose was a blonde-haired beauty, an angel he never felt he deserved, clad in a flowing black dress and silver jewellery. They had married late last year at twenty-two and were forever lost in each other's eyes; now they held hands across the table and awaited their company.

"We've been here forever; you don't think something has happened, do you?" asked Rose. As much as she could sit here and wait all night, it had been an hour now, and though the scrawny, high-voiced waiter was polite, he kept asking for their order.

"Have you met Drake? Being fashionably late is a trait of his," Nathan replied, well aware of his best friend's inadequacy.

"I often wonder how he ties his own shoes in the morning," replied Rose before taking a sip of wine.

"Until recently his butler tied them."

Rose tried not to laugh for fear of red wine exiting her nose and covering the white tablecloth, but there was nothing she could do. She took a napkin stop herself, then she scrunched it hard and threw it at Nathan, but it missed. He ducked, it went over the back of his chair and landed on the head of a rather large bald man, mid-dessert. The man glared around the booth, but Rose and Nathan picked up their menus and played the fool.

They both sniggered and Nathan lent in to take her hand. He looked around the room at all the old photographs of the nearby city streets telling cobbled tales in black and white of a different place and time.

"I don't mind waiting, I could sit here forever with you."

"Nathan." Rose almost coughed up her wine again.

"I find it very hard to sit here with you when you do that thing!"

"What thing?"

"Just … just …" Rose looked back at him and supposed it was love for everything about him. He was strong, kind and had a good sense of humour. It was all the more special when he could be so stern around everyone else, and he worked so damned hard to get where he needed to be, despite his circumstances. "Do you remember when Drake forgot his trousers for the morning sports class and had to wear those old gym shorts?"

"I do," replied Nathan.

"Do you remember when he started that fight with the year above, and you had to save him?"

"Unfortunately, I do," said Nathan with that smile.

"I don't know how he ever got Evelyn to agree to a date, to be honest."

"He uses very big words, won't take no for an answer, and, let's face it, he's funny."

It was at that moment that Evelyn entered and stole the room, a young civil servant of the age of twenty, with curly brown hair, bronze skin and a wide smile. She wore a satin emerald dress that complemented her complexion and accentuated crystal-blue eyes.

Evelyn was accompanied by Drake Owen. Drake was short, stout, and boyish, with dirty blonde hair. He left most people wondering he how he had ever tricked her into dating him, and the answer was his charisma. They walked hand in hand as if caught in a dream, almost bypassing the waiter who showed them to their table.

"Well, well, well!" said Drake, taking the attention of the happy couple at the table, who shot up in anticipation of their guests.

"Here they are – Evelyn, you look beautiful as ever this evening, though it's not like you to be late," he said, greeting her with a kiss on the cheek. She seemed ecstatic, excited by something. She approached Rose and lost all sense of formality as they held each other tight – the pair were like sisters. They had all been at the same school, though Evelyn was a few years younger.

Nathan extended a hand to Drake, which was met with a raised eyebrow and a moody scowl before Drake jumped to embrace him. Nathan wasn't one to enjoy such affection, and hesitated, but Drake knew when his friend needed it.

They took some time to shuffle in and get comfy as the waiter watched with polite impatience, checking his watch three times before coming to take their order.

"May I get you something to drink?" asked the smartly dressed waiter, with his thin moustache and tightly wound bow tie.

"What do you have?" asked Drake, somewhat overcome with excitement and slightly red-faced from the heat in his grey suit.

"That depends, sir, on what is right for this beautiful madame."

The group chuckled at the waiter's attempted flattery, and Drake took a moment to choose. "We will take the most expensive bottle of champagne on the menu, old boy."

Nathan looked up in surprise; he was no stranger to the finer things, but still he hated overspending. The price in sovereigns was five hundred, and it was quite a bottle for a Thursday night in the city, even for a successful banker like Drake.

"Drake, I don't think that –"

"Nonsense, we need to celebrate," said Drake with a large smile. He giggled to himself, and before Nathan could ask why, Evelyn lifted her hand and presented the glistening rock on her finger. She blushed, having never been the type of girl who liked to show off in the way the ring intended her to; in fact, it made her feel rather insecure. Like Nathan, she hadn't come from wealth and their schooling had been funded by scholarships.

The shock of seeing the ring made Rose's jaw drop, and Nathan, despite them having half spoken of the occasion for months and even years, stood in surprise, almost knocking over the table. "Drake, you finally did it! I never thought you would have the courage," he said. "Waiter, bring *two* bottles!"

"Oh, Evelyn! I have so many questions – have you set a date? What did your parents say? Can I be a bridesmaid?" Rose could hardly contain herself; to see her best friends look to tie the knot after so many ups and downs raised her spirits no end. Evelyn laughed as the ring glistened and she looked down at a bright and promising future. "Well, I wanted you to be my maid of honour," she confessed. Rose made no attempt to hide her excitement.

"This calls for a toast!" Nathan declared as the waiter poured each of them a glass. "To Evelyn and Drake, the closest friends we've ever had, and to a bright future," he continued; and with a clink it was done. Rose spoke of the wedding preparations in detail as Evelyn tried to keep up. After a few glasses, Drake spoke about the business of Sovereign banking, the strained international relationship with the Union's financial stronghold Fortune, and the city of Favour, as Nathan listened, desperately trying to pay attention. He knew the Far East and Western states were still at war, and it was foolish to think the Kingdom Isle would ever go to war with the Union over some financial dispute.

As the evening wore on, they shared a delicious seafood platter to start, Nathan ordered the linguine for the main, and many laughs and glasses of champagne followed until each of them was stuffed. Nathan was slightly distant – happy but distant; his mind drifted to other things as Drake recounted the trials of nine-to-five office life. For Nathan, Monday was deployment somewhere classified, for an undisclosed amount of time, and many did not make it back alive. As well-meaning words and wishes crossed the table, he could not help but think of the danger ahead. Drake tapped him on the arm to break his daze, looked up with dizzy eyes and asked, "Shall we go for a cigarette?"

Nathan followed him and the next minute they found themselves in the alleyway lit by an old flickering streetlight, with live music from a concert hall down the road providing the aural backdrop. Drake passed one over and they lit up, taking in the relief and the cold winter air.

"Is everything okay, Nathan?"

Nathan looked back at his friend. He never wanted to bore him with his worries, having always maintained a self-sufficient way about him, and being so obsessive over his demeanour. His stern look let nothing go, and he put on a brave face while adjusting his posture.

"No, no. I'm fine."

"So, you're deployed Monday, I'm sorry to hear –"

"It's my job."

"I know. But I just could never imagine either of us as soldiers – well, especially me. There's always room for you at my father's bank if needs be."

Nathan looked down at his plump friend and chuckled; he didn't take handouts. Having spent so long working this hard, he couldn't stop now. He took a drag and shrugged, a polite decline.

Drake looked around quite sheepishly, as if to check if there was anyone around. "I have to ask you something."

"Go on …"

Drake leant in to whisper with worry in his eyes, as if about to second-guess himself. "Do you think I'm making the right decision?"

"About what? Marrying Evelyn? God, it's probably the best decision you have ever made … but she is way out of your league."

Drake laughed and wiped his clammy brow; he admired his friend's honesty. Sometimes it felt as if Nathan was the only person in the world he trusted.

Everyone else just seemed out for money, except for Evelyn of course: she could live poor and broke; as long as she was helping people, she didn't rightly care.

"I wanted to ask you something else ... I wanted to see if you would do me the honour of – of being my best man?"

Nathan looked at him with a serious face, but it quickly turned to a smile; they were brothers, there was nothing that could ever come between them.

"I thought you would ask your university lot, like Arthur or Toby. Drake, I-I don't know what to say. I –"

"Just say yes. Cranes, man, this has been harder than bloody proposing!"

"*Yes*. Yes ... but ... but what if I don't come back ..."

It was peculiar for Nathan to say something so harrowing. It wasn't like him at all to show such doubt and lay out his greatest worry for his best friend to hear.

"You? You always come back. You're tough, mean. Look at that firm brow and stern jawline. Remember the time you had to carry me down that western mountain?"

"Nevis? That was more of a hill."

"What about when our canoe capsized and you swam me to shore, only to carry me a mile back to camp?"

"It was two miles, and you said you had pneumonia ..."

"Remember when we were jumped by ten scally-wags outside the fish and chip shop?"

"There were five."

"Still, five on two, the odds were against us, but we showed them a thing or two, didn't we, old chap!" Drake attempted to shadow-box, almost falling over in the process, as he lacked any speed or balance.

"*I* showed them a thing or two."

"Well, I was there for moral support."

After reminiscing, they flicked their cigarettes to the ground before crushing them. Nathan took one last look at the blue and pink sunset behind the thatched roofs of the city and wondered what the future would hold. It was at that moment that an unexpected hand came down on his shoulder from behind. He turned to see who it was. A very tall (given that Nathan was six foot three himself) bald man dressed in black leant over him. He was scarred, haggard, and Nathan thought that sneaking up on people probably wasn't the best career for him.

"Mister Sahl, is it? I need a word," he said in a deep, gruff voice as Nathan looked up at him.

"I think you've made a mistake."

"You look like your father, you do – but half the man, or half the man before …" grunted the stranger, and Nathan held himself back, gritting his teeth.

"Twenty minutes, now or never," the stranger added, before he turned to walk away. He started whistling.

Nathan turned to Drake with unusual concern and lost his calm for a moment. "Cover for me, say I'm stuck on a call about Monday."

Drake studied his friend for a moment. "Are you sure? We can take him, if we need to."

Nathan nodded, and so his friend went back inside. He turned to follow the gruff, bald man down the dark alleyway, walking a few steps behind and gripping his combat pistol. Down through the darkness they went until the large man passed him some black sunglasses. He knew that this was the moment, that it was all real.

"Put these on," the stranger said, and Nathan did. He could not see a thing. The man took him by the arm and guided him to the edge of the pavement. A car pulled up and he was pushed inside. After being wedged into place between two giants, they took off slowly down the street.

"You can take the glasses off now, Mister Sahl," came a light mysterious whisper. Nathan took them off and was overcome by the brightness of a light above a figure up ahead. He could only just make out the outline of a fitted grey suit and hat. Sitting to Nathan's right was the large bald man, and to the left another. The gruff man alongside him revealed a service pistol and popped each bullet from the chamber onto the floor. Nathan felt his pocket and realised it was his gun.

"We don't have much time, so allow me to be brief. We know you have been looking for us, Mister Sahl, and we are a very hard organisation to find. However, we are everywhere, and I promise it was very easy to find *you*." The figure leant forward and revealed a large, cat-like smile. "I know you have waited half your life for this moment."

"So, the Ministry of Men exists; my father didn't lie after all."

"He didn't lie, but he broke the code and died all

the same, for reasons beyond our control. Do you believe in fate, Mister Sahl?"

"What does it matter?"

"Oh, it matters. There's a hint of madness in your family; how hard will you try to fight it?"

"I will never be like my father."

"Indeed, and we would never place the sins of the father upon the son, but I will tell you this. There are things beyond your control that we intend to hide, things that would shock your very being. I am here to offer you a chance to change the world. The Ministry of Men is a network, an order, and there are many of us most powerful, some you will never know exist." The large man next to Nathan opened a satchel to reveal a thick wad of documents. "There is only one chance to join us. Say no and we will never cross paths again; but say yes and your life will change forever. You have about nine minutes to get back inside the restaurant before your darling wife Rose starts asking questions, so please do hurry."

Nathan took a moment in the blinding light to decide what to say. He tried to keep a level head after the champagne, but there was no time to think.

"Yes."

"Then sign here, here, here, here, here, here and here – oh, and here." Nathan signed each and every piece of paper without so much as reading a page, keen to rebuild his father's reputation and their family name: a chance of redemption. The binder snapped shut and the ogre handed Nathan back his pistol before prompting him to put the glasses back on. The car slammed to a halt, the door opened, and Nathan began to shuffle out.

"Take ten steps forward before taking off the glasses, and watch the puddle – oh, and Nathan –"

"Yes?"

"Treasure every second, it won't last forever."

A large unfriendly arm pushed him out of the vehicle and he stumbled in his blind state. He took ten slow steps whilst looking down at the ground to check for the aforementioned puddle.

"There's nothing worse than wet socks," he muttered whilst moving forward. When he took off the dark glasses and adjusted his eyes, he was standing at the edge of a large puddle. With a spring in his step and a smile, Nathan marched back down the alley to meet his friends, worried sick about how they would be. Soon he saw the lantern at the end of the alleyway, and the lovely thatched black and white restaurant. He felt on top of the world and shone his million-dollar smile just before his brogue crashed into a large, icy puddle. He sighed, laughed, and shook it off, reassuring himself that it didn't matter. His military career was bound for greatness, his part to play would be grand, for there was no finer secret establishment than the Ministry of Men, and even if there was, he would never know.

3

THE COMMONS

Ten years later, much had changed in the once great city of Sovereign. A population crisis, economic collapse, mass starvation and lack of resources had made the whole of Kingdom Isle crumble in bittersweet denial. The North had consumed itself to its skeleton; neglected by its government, the military was failing to keep control, and its lawless people fought in the street for scraps. The South hung on only in its capital. Only Sovereign remained, only Sovereign was safe. The once proud home of kings somehow managed to keep the nation going, lie after lie.

The central Capital District once gleamed with wealth and glamour, but now the walls, checkpoints and police lines took away most of its shine. It was a false spectacle, surrounded by a mass of poverty and discontent. No matter how hard the Capital District tried to separate itself from its failures, nothing could be done about the smell of the surrounding boroughs. Their troubles were ignored. There were no solutions, only longer curfews, more arrests and severe punishments. Those with wealth didn't want to see all this but it was too close to ignore. The most obvious signs of failure at the heart of Sovereign were the large concrete walls, the checkpoints close to the Old Abbey and what was once Bakersville. Everything beyond the line was the Commons now. What was once a proud place of successful businesses saw recession, riots and looting. The smell of flooded sewers, pollution and poverty took hold, and for ten long years everything was dark and grey.

On what was once Bakersville's busy Market Street a man stood entranced, staring into nothing. Hollow cheekbones protruded on account of his illness, his blond hair was withered and dry, and his red eyes hid behind circular thick-rimmed glasses. His clothes were tattered, and much too big, as he had shrunk with time. His posture was poor, and his weight was carried by a walking stick, which further bespoke an unusual decline for a man in his late twenties.

His name, if he could remember it, was Samuel James Royle, and if he ever met anyone who knew him, they would call him Sam. He was a very different man to the Sam of old, so different that all they appeared to share was their name. He stared on, trying to regain focus and not draw any unwanted attention to his momentary lapse. He was an easy target lacking strength, speed and wit. His therapist had reminded him it was due to the accident; one he could not remember but which had cursed him with a cruel mental and physical illness all the same. He had no personality and no humour. His bones ached and trembled; even the slightest knock could cause them to break. Every morning was agony until he swallowed his pills of various sizes and colours. Blue for the headaches, red for fatigue, green for his bones and yellow for his breathing. The physical pain was nothing compared to the mental, though. For as calm as he was, he had no memory of getting here. Suffering from frequent blips, he went from one place to the next with no memory of what had happened in between.

Placing his feeble, shaking hand in his pocket, he withdrew a notepad and pencil before beginning to scribble on a page dated the 3rd of January 2095. He checked for notes of other blips; there had been two today already, so he crossed them out and scribbled down number three. The only other words on the page were a name: Doctor Janet Fielding. He looked back to see the crumbling therapist's office and tried to fight off another momentary lapse. She had told him to breathe and close his eyes, to listen. There were sirens, laughter, screams and shouts, glass smashing in the distance. He smelt smoke, damp, mould and pollution staining the air. When he opened his eyes, he saw the decrepit concrete street, the smashed windows, the pot-holed pavement. Aimless crowds gathered in rags, and people lay down with closed eyes, hooked on *glass*, a toxic and addictive mind-altering substance. It was cold, it was wretched, and it was real.

A speck of rain hit Sam's eye. He looked up at the dark polluted clouds; evening was coming soon, and the streets would not be safe. Outside the doctor's office he must have met with her most recently, but the blips had taken that away. It would have been another pointless session focused on his illusions. Flicking back through the notepad, past scribbles of numbers and notes, poorly written fragments filled the pages with words to remind himself of basic needs, such as *eat* and *sleep*. He flicked past shaky drawings produced by a trembling hand. Some were of dark buildings like the Asylum. It made him shudder. Others showed ghost-like figures, a man covered in spirals; a woman with no face was the most frequent. He tried to remember but there were no memories.

Doctor Fielding had told him the Asylum was real and that he'd spent years there after a horrific car accident. The woman, however, could have been anyone, and that scared him the most. Doctor Fielding also theorised an addiction to glass, a substance that tore apart the lives of many. She said he was a frequent user before the crash and was repressing his memories through guilt about those he'd lost. The drawings were a way for him to escape, but he could never remember drawing anything. The woman was a metaphor for the life he'd lost – his mother, perhaps. Whenever he tried to remember, a trembling in his brain cut through him, another lapse.

There it was, the blistering pain and blindness. Falling onto all fours, he dropped the notepad from his shaking hands; his glasses were gone, too. Searching desperately, he tried to breathe, and to observe his surroundings. Blind and alone amidst the business of this broken street, he was nothing. No one would stop to help him now, for those days were gone. He scrabbled around on the cold wet concrete, hyperventilating through his weak frame. All hope was lost until a pair of finely polished black brogues met his eyes and an umbrella tapped on the ground.

Time seemed to cease.

Another illusion, he thought, as the figure pulled him to his feet. The figure's head was down, and covered with a grey hat matching the suit it wore. The figure passed back the notepad, pushed it into Sam's top pocket and patted it twice before returning his scratched spectacles.

"Be more careful next time, and get yourself an umbrella," said the figure with a blurred smile, in a somewhat sinister tone, before turning and walking away. The voice was high, sickly sweet even, and a cold shiver took hold as Sam saw the back of the figure disappear into the distance, a stranger dressed in grey, shrouded by a city just the same. Desperate not to panic, he tried to control his breathing, for the attacks were fierce and the hallucinations relentless. Such episodes were frequent; the last thing he needed was another one on his file, another visit from community control, another journey to the Asylum.

It began to rain, and he remembered he was far from home. It was late. It would be curfew soon, but the bus was close. He needed to get home, so he kept his head down and began to hobble, aided by his stick. Sirens filled the air, a constant feature of the city, another background noise to add to the shouts, the alarms, the chanting and the flames. There were groups gathered on every corner, with no jobs and nothing to do but sit and smoke glass. Everyone was going mad. Groups of children were frequent, for the schools had closed years before. In an hour the smart few would go inside but those who dared to riot would remain to take out their frustrations on the city.

The buildings that lined either side of the street were once a retail haven but were now derelict, stained and sour. Only a few days had gone by since the last shop he passed had been broken into and emptied. Sovereign was a sad shadow of its former self, a metaphor for the wider state of affairs. It was cold, and colder still for him. Standing blankly in a zombie-like state, the last lapse had turned into a headache that crushed him. He fought it off while limping down the road, every step a struggle, until he had covered the very short distance to the bus stop. Remaining distant despite the business around him, people waited, and the sounds of the city took over as Sam feared the cold of another lapse – it was only a matter of time. He felt all but buried, until someone barged into him, almost knocking him down.

"Sorry, mate," said a gruff man in blue overalls, with desperation in his voice. He was covered in grease and smelled like fumes. Sam deduced that he must be some sort of mechanic, but a closer inspection revealed a smuggler's tattoo on his knuckle: a skeleton in a coffin, the sign of the feared and mighty grave smugglers. If Sam could have, he would have turned and run. Instead, he hesitated, his mind too slow to react, but he knew that the mechanic had been traumatised by something, or was in a hurry at least. Sam was afraid to speak, for those around him might call community control, and the Asylum would have him once more. But the mechanic kept staring, awaiting a response as the crowd moved away.

"Don't worry about it," Sam muttered, his quiet reply lost amidst the noise.

Down the street on the right, two community control officers were looking in every direction for someone. Sam could guess who that was, but he could not alert them, he wouldn't wish that on anyone. He shook his head, cursing the illusion, but the man in the blue shirt stayed, muttering to himself with a sense of impatience. Thankfully the bus pulled up, putting itself between them, and Sam could be out of there and back in the cramped, damp flat he struggled to call home. Two pills and the man would fizzle away, he knew that for sure.

It was hard to climb on, raise a shaking hand, scan the pass from his pocket, pass the driver and keep his head down. He shied away from the strangers ahead but felt their eyes following him. The poor, the ill-looking glassheads, those who struggled to walk. Most people tended not to take the bus, for somehow walking was safer. Sam shuffled along the rusted hulk and took a damp seat at the back, looking up to check for the mechanic once more. His head was hunched over, a few rows in front. It was easy to stare before the piercing feeling took over, and Sam did everything to hold on, desperate not to blip again. He wanted to point, scream and shout, but the last thing he needed was trouble with community control. *I can't go back, not again*, he thought as he looked outside.

The bus passed burnt-out restaurants and shops that held a blurred sense of nostalgia. He had been here before, in a different life. It was impossible to remember since the accident; but still when he passed such things he couldn't help but smile: for a moment it felt like he knew something. But all too soon those positive thoughts were swept away by a piercing headache. Every time he came close to remembering anything significant, the pain began. The brain repressed it all. A shooting pain: something always brought it back.

The bus slammed to a halt, sending its passengers into shock. In the headlights stood a man with his right hand raised as rain poured down over his large black hooded coat. On the coat was the insignia of the Sovereign crown in a circle of thorns; he was a community control officer. A cold and unfriendly face stained with a thousand bad deeds shone in the headlights. In his own time, he walked round to the doors with a brooding swagger and pulled out a stun baton.

The officer tapped the door as two others joined his side. The doors didn't open right away, for the bus driver had frozen. Everyone was afraid, nobody dared move as they all sat waiting and wondering who was next. The doors opened and the officer walked up each step with a heavy thud; everyone was quiet and kept their heads down. Detentions were a regular occurrence in the Sovereign Commons; many had disappeared. The officer stared at the bus driver with cold, unforgiving eyes. His hands shook upon the wheel as the officer reached into his pocket and pulled out a photograph.

"Have you seen this man?" he asked, cold yet calm, appraising every passenger with his haunting glare. There were several men on board with their heads down, praying it wasn't them, for no one in the Commons was innocent.

"I … I don't know," the bus driver whimpered.

"He was seen protesting yesterday and threw a petrol bomb at one of our boys," the officer said, loud enough for all to hear, a smug sickness in his voice. He looked around to see anyone who might be making eye contact; if he wasn't here, someone would be made an example of. There was a wicked sense of enjoyment that sadly all in his position shared: it was hard not to enjoy the intimidation, the authority, the easy pay, in a world where most had nothing.

"Look at me!" he shouted, and everyone present raised their heads. The officer, trained to smell fear, stared at the mechanic.

Remain calm, try to breathe, Sam told himself.

The officer took a step closer and clicked the button on his baton; a pulse of blue static electricity followed, bringing harsh memories to all who had seen one before. Most had seen someone take a beating and had a few burns themselves.

The officer nodded to his accomplices as they approached the fifth row and dragged the mechanic up by his collar. "No, no, no," he said in desperation, "Please, I have children." He held on to anything he could, but a harsh knee met his gut. When he went down, another sharp pain in Sam's brain matched the fall. They dragged the mechanic from his seat and down the bus as he protested. For a moment he locked eyes with Sam. He begged, he pleaded, and then the anger took him: the injustice of it all.

"You pigs, you fucking pigs!" he shouted, making his biggest mistake, giving them what they wanted, an excuse. Community control officers were corrupt, vile; they took bribes and stole what little they could from the poor – and they adored an excuse, a reason to pounce, any sign of disrespect, no matter how small. It was obvious to Sam then: illusions were never of this size – so he knew that the supposed illusion was a man after all.

"I want you all to see this! Don't move this bus!" shouted the first officer, foaming at the mouth as the others dragged their victim along the filth-ridden floor, out of the door and onto the road. The officer in charge walked back toward the bus driver and gave him a pat on the shoulder before taking the few steps out into the rain. Everyone remained silent and looked out of the window, not daring to look away.

Throwing the man to the floor, they booted him in the back of the legs. The harsh ground grazed his hands and knees. The officer charged his baton; blue sparks jittered in the rain. One mighty swing and the baton hit the back of the man's head. The shock made him spasm. The smell of burning hair took over as they beat him again and again. He whimpered and gasped, then silence followed. Unconscious now, his head spilt blood, his face deep enough in the puddles to drown.

Don't look away, don't look away.

The officer turned back to the bus doors. "Go on now, piss off!" he shouted.

They handcuffed and dragged what was now a ghost over to the squad car as the bus doors slowly creaked to a close and it took off again. The whole bus stayed silent, afraid, but there were no tears. They had seen similar things happen before; it was just another reminder of the world they lived in. A world so desperate that those who had once sworn to protect had forgotten their Sovereign oaths. He wanted to feel something, anything, but even though he knew the man was real, he felt nothing but the ache; the medication was wearing off and he needed more.

The bus rolled away and in the darkness came something to make his head all the sorer. Leaning on a green bench and holding an umbrella was the figure in grey. The brim of its hat hid the figure's identity in shadow, revealing only a pale frown. The figure held an orange marigold flower and whispered a funeral prayer. Shaking his head and rubbing his eyes, a shiver met Sam's spine and the man was gone. At least he was an illusion.

A half hour journey of solemn silence followed. Sam passed the time in worrying about the man in grey and the ghost. He found himself obsessing, hyperventilating, shaking, and in need of pills to reset for another day. Whilst he wrestled with his own mind, he failed to notice that the bus had stopped and was empty. The driver had seen him before maybe a hundred times, but he didn't speak. Instead he waited in silence, taking a break, for this was the end of the line. Standing when his knees allowed him to get to his feet, Sam shuffled down the aisle and out onto the street.

It was a short walk to his bedsit, but it seemed so long. The air stank of sewage and the night was growing dark. As quickly as he could, he hobbled up the steps and made his way to the main door. It took time to find the key and longer to open up. The light flickered on and he saw the stained, once white walls, and smelt the joys of poor plumbing. Climbing the long staircase to the fourth floor took forever. With frequent breaks, holding onto the handrail to stay steady, he at last arrived. Another lock on another door, and with great struggle it was open.

His bedsit was small, awkward and crooked, stained and brown. The bed was practically in the kitchen, and the kitchen in his living area, and so on. The only other room was a wet room with a shower above the toilet. There were big juicy rats, but he wasn't fast enough to catch them. It was untidy, dusty and damp. The place lacked any personality; if you asked Sam, he would not remember the landlord, how he paid or why he was there.

Standing by the bed, he opened various packets of pills and swallowed them down with a glass of water. He looked over at his chair; the reading lamp was still on, and there were stacks of drawings and the few books he had managed to keep hold of, which he couldn't read but refused to burn. There were no photographs, ornaments or souvenirs of travel.

He picked up the notepad: *eat* was scribbled on it, and underlined three times. Sam took the few steps to the cupboard, rummaged, and picked up a half tin of beans. Trembling, he checked his watch. It was 7.00 p.m. so he set an alarm for half an hour to battle the blips – if he suffered another time lapse his watch would disturb him. He collapsed in his old tartan wingback chair; there was a half-finished glass of cheap gin from yesterday on the windowsill. *Jackpot*, he thought, and after a few small sips he was out. He left the beans on the side; after today he had forgotten to eat them.

He awoke to the bleeping of his watch. Its noise swirled around his head; his eyes fogged over, but he felt oddly painless. It was a dream, and he was unable to fight, unable to move. He looked down at his watch, struggling to make out the blurred figures. It said 10.03 p.m. Heavy eyes moved to the window, and sure enough, down below in the rain was the one with the umbrella, dressed in the same grey suit and hat, but the pale face didn't smile anymore.

A sharp fear took him over, a terrible sense of dread, as the one in grey mouthed something. *"Good luck,"* he said, *"good luck."*

The door slammed and the noise cascaded through Sam's mind. Two men entered, dressed in black, one tall and one plump. Sam tried to scream, then tried to move but could do nothing. One of the men placed a gun on the side table to his right. Defiantly trying to stand with all his might, Sam fell forward on all fours.

"It smells like shit in here," said the tall one.

"We've buried bodies, and you think this sorry fool's flat smells like shit?" asked the shorter one as he crouched down to address Sam properly. He placed a hand on Sam's cheek. "It'll be over soon."

The other grabbed Sam's collar and with one hand, and with ease sat him back upright before tying his hands and legs together. Sam's attempt to talk came out slurred as the room span around him. "W-why?" he whispered, unable to say more.

"Because you're the one they need, Samuel James Royle."

The name … the name of a stranger, the name of a ghost and the name of a past long forgotten. The words shot through his brain like a spark, ending in hideous pain, and that was the last thing Sam heard …

4

DECISIONS

At the edge of the Commons, past high fences, guard towers and roadblocks, was Evercrest. It was home to politicians, bankers and bureaucrats with butlers and nannies. Cars filled the roads but only officers and chauffeurs would drive them; there was also a small private school. Here, grand apartments of grey Cotswold stone stretched high above the cityscape, enclosing beautiful private gardens, lavish and well-tended, which, even on such a cold and misty evening, looked beautiful. On the rooftop overlooking the garden most grand was a man on the edge of the free world.

Nathan Sahl was not much different to the man he had been ten years prior, having aged well. He was broader, but he still had his thick dark brown hair. He stood looking immaculate, dressed in a dark grey suit, black overcoat and leather gloves, embracing the cold as his breath misted in the crisp white air.

There was no need for formal military attire

anymore; the past ten years had been kind to him in many ways, but despite his good fortune, lines of worry surrounded his once hopeful eyes. He stared into the beautiful garden below with a sense of impatience and frustration. It was one of his favourite spots to think things over, to look down and plan his next move, but for once in his life he didn't have one. Having played every move with caution, no matter what he did, the pieces had turned to fickle pawns. Nathan's dream of being appointed Chief of Defence, the most important role in the Kingdom Isle, had faded as it approached fruition. The closer his career drove him towards the position, the less he wanted to be there. It had taken the unexpected demise of his predecessor, Baylor Frankfurt, a gluttonous oaf full of character and charm, although beneath the surface a self-centred and somewhat callous monster. If Nathan had been told statistics and not based things on unfounded rumours, he would never have stood for election as Chief. In the face of war and terrorism, Baylor had killed hundreds of rioters and protesters, and then in turn innocent civilians, without trial, whilst the Ministry of Men, and most importantly, the Kingdom Central Government, did nothing to stop him.

Nathan had tried to do everything to help his struggling Kingdom, but the country was falling down around him and the government he'd bled for was falling too. The weight bore down upon his shoulders as accusations of tyranny were made behind closed doors. Blurred lines were being falsely drawn between himself and Baylor. Enemies were everywhere, as Baylor had been a puppet of his generals – generals that were also members of the Ministry of Men, the secret society Nathan had worked his whole life for. He'd bled for them as well, yet he was still at the bottom of the ladder. Now the Kingdom's government had asked him to give evidence at trial, but Nathan knew what they really wanted. They wanted him to walk into the Old Abbey, pass the honour guards unarmed, and take responsibility for his predecessor. He would not, he could not, and so, as he stood, his brow lowered in concern while he surveyed his city. Desperate times called for desperate measures.

"How long have you been up here?" he asked, for behind him, leaning casually, hands on hips, was a tall slender woman in a nano-armoured suit, her light grey hair tightly pulled back. She had hypnotic golden eyes and black lipstick, which contrasted with a pale complexion. Nathan knew it wasn't worth asking how she'd got onto the roof past gates and guards who shot on sight, for he knew the answer.

"Long enough to see your troubles; I can spot that spoilt male broodiness anywhere," she replied, standing even more upright, before coming forward to get a better look at him. "They said you were tall and strong, but no one ever said you were handsome. Moody exterior, soft interior; looks like you have the entire package, Chief Sahl."

"I could have you vanish, and no one would bat an eye."

"Vanish? Oh, go ahead, take me away, I'm *shaking*," said the stranger, holding her wrists together as though ready to be cuffed; and then, as if into thin air, she disappeared. Nathan looked around, having never known such technology. He listened closely for footsteps. "I find men of comfort lose their sharp edge," she replied as Nathan turned to find her standing to his left.

"I'm sharper and quicker than you think."

"You couldn't catch me if you tried – too rusty; and when was the last time you stretched? Besides, what would my employer say if you took me in, he wouldn't like that at all."

Nathan reminisced about how fast he used to be on the battlefield, in his own armour. He could catch her, he could catch anyone; but then the memories of bloodshed made him shudder. "Neither of us are here for small talk," he said.

"Well, you know who I am, that I crossed the Union, crossed the Channel, passed through your broken city without being seen or heard – and all just for you."

"How sweet of the Union's Claw to do that for me."

"That is what they call me," she said with a shrug, before taking a slight smug bow."

"Others call you Cat."

"Careful, Chief, I have sharp claws, and I'll scratch out a dog's eyes if it comes too close." Razor claws glimmered from the assassin's suit, but Nathan was unfazed. Calm in any situation, he knew that her real name was in fact Caterina.

"What is it that you want?"

"That's just it, Nathan, it isn't what *I* want, it's

about what *you* want, what my employer wants, and how we can get you out of this little pickle."

As much as Nathan tried to hide his worries, he couldn't. He leant back upon the roof's edge and tried to think clearly. It was hard, given his lack of sleep; he could not fathom her words and so he turned to rest both his hands on the parapet and looked out upon his city once more. Cat took a few steps toward the edge but remained far from him.

"It's beautiful, despite it falling apart, but it isn't as beautiful as Purity, as Pinnacle," she said.

Cat was right: the Union state of Purity was a gargantuan paradise, the capital Pinnacle its pride and joy, and despite its right-wing totalitarian leadership, it was the future, where Sovereign was the past.

"Purity isn't home."

"Home is where you make it. In Purity you can have riches: fame and wealth, safe travel for your family, anything else your heart desires. Besides, you're ruined. If your government doesn't kill you then the Ministry of Men surely will – unless we strike at them first."

Nathan turned to her, to golden eyes he didn't trust. Everyone had to earn his trust, and as a Unionist, Cat would never get the opportunity. He didn't quail in her presence like the rest; he was calm and level-headed. "You speak of treason."

"There can be no treason against what is already trying to kill you. Think of your wife, think of your soon to be born son."

Her words were a weapon that shot through his heart. Nathan would be a father very soon and Rose was his entire world. As much as he didn't want her to be, Cat was right. They were not safe; they would never be safe unless he did whatever he could to make it so.

"We will give you soldiers, eliminate all your enemies – our enemies – and you will have a seat upon the Union Council, all for –"

Nathan knew what they wanted, what they yearned for. It was easy for him to calculate his enemies' thinking, but whether the prize could be provided at such short notice was far from certain. It might not be easy, but it was the only way.

"The Titan," he said, and Cat's eyes lit up at its very mention. The Titan was the largest flying military vehicle in the world. It was a giant spherical base, a weapon that could bring any nation to its knees. Faced by an energy crisis, the Unionists wanted its renewable energy and its artificial intelligence programme. There was only one problem: two scientists had shut it down when they ended the Mech Wars. There was only one way to start it again and that was near impossible – but he had no choice.

"If you agree to bring High Councillor Rogan the Titan, we will put an end to this nightmare tomorrow. How long do you need to get it operational?"

"A week," Nathan replied, biting his tongue.

"You have forty-eight hours."

That was impossible, it couldn't be done, but he did not so much as blink an eye. *There's no other way*, he thought. He thought of Rose, he thought of the child. There was no future here; they would put him in chains and make him watch as the nation consumed itself to ashes. What the country needed was order, and only he could give it.

Cat put a hand behind her and pulled an envelope from her carry pack. "Tomorrow, at seven in the evening, when the cathedral bell rings it will begin. Get your armour and keep your best men close. Issue the orders, put on the headset and await the call from Chief Councillor Rogan." She passed him an envelope and a small micro-headset. "If you're with us, place something red on your office windowsill tonight; if not, I will give you a day's head start. I'll be gentle with her, but with you I can make no promises." On Cat's last word, her facemask formed before she turned and began to run to the other side of the roof. Nathan watched as the invisible messenger, the assassin, disappeared, and he was left alone.

The same feeling of anxiety took hold again despite his strength. It was hard not to worry about Rose, about everyone. When Nathan looked down at his hands, he couldn't help but see blood. They were never made for politics, only war, and he would rather use them to crush his sharp-tongued enemies. Cat's unexpected appearance and offer echoed in his mind but there was no time to stop. Taking a deep breath in the cool air to prepare himself, he saw in the distance a man sitting on a bench between two willow trees. Nathan approached the high wall and looked down the sharp drop. He took the fire escape down, determined not to go through the house and disturb Rose on a night like tonight. It was high, but he wasn't scared of heights. He passed their bedroom and moments later the living room. She was still there, still safe from the chaos outside. Down the ladder he went, scaling it to the bottom, desperate to meet an old friend. It had been far too long since he had seen Drake; they had grown distant of late in many ways. Nathan had grown cold, more stern, whereas Drake had never quite left his boisterous party lifestyle behind him.

At the bottom, Nathan's feet met stone. He crossed the garden following the winding path that split the lawn in two. Low lights cast a large shadow behind him as he slowly made his way. Hiding his concern, he passed the darkness of flowerbeds covered in frost; the light was reflecting upon the rose bushes, setting them apart from everything else, a contrasting blend of Union red and Sovereign white. He stopped for a moment and picked the one most appropriate, placing it carefully in his side pocket. He kept moving past hedgerows and approached his old friend, who sat hunched upon the park bench.

Drake's metabolism had caught up with him: stouter now, his olive eyes were dark, and his dirty blond hair was losing its colour and thickness. Pink from the cold, he had been waiting outside a little too long. He wore a navy suit, too large for him, and it made him look even more like the overdressed and over-worked banker he had accidentally fashioned himself into. Even worse, he seemed slightly intoxicated, but at this point Nathan didn't know whether that was just the affect sobriety had on an addict.

"I was wondering if you were going to show," Drake

said, as Nathan took a seat alongside him and they both looked out towards the fountain.

"I had another meeting that over-ran," Nathan replied. He wanted to apologise, but there was just so much on his mind. Saying sorry wasn't really his way, and instead he withdrew two cherry cigars from his pocket, along with an engraved, rose-gold hip flask containing the finest aged port. He went to pass Drake one of the sweet-smelling sticks and Drake passed back a matching rose-gold lighter that Nathan had gifted him on his wedding day. The mutual exchange had brought an understanding between the two friends that was unbroken by time or tyranny.

Nathan struck the light, lit both cigars and passed one back. He took a swig of port to wash it down before passing the bottle to his friend. It warmed Drake a little but there was sadness in his eyes, a look of concern that he could not shake. Nathan could have spotted it a mile off, for he knew him so well.

"Absolute treat – the Nathan I knew would never have splashed out on something so sweet." Drake's words held the same old warmth, but there was something ever so strange about his voice; he had lost his boyish charm and instead it trembled.

"It was a gift. Is everything alright, Drake?"

"Me? Alright? Is everything alright?" Drake paused for a moment and let out a mighty sigh whilst trying to hold it together. He winced and rubbed his eyes. "I've lost it all." Nathan looked at him unsure of what to say. "I said *all* – all our money."

Nathan didn't pretend to be surprised; he knew.

This day had come close before, but Drake had always worked his way out of things. Big cigars and games of cards were his forte. He loved to gamble – something about the risk, the dice, and the rush when he won big. It had never ended with a rush, though, and Drake Owen had lost it all.

"I can get your money back, every sovereign."

Drake laughed, shook his head and finally turned to his friend to look him in the eye. He took the hip flask from Nathan's hand and took another swig before wiping it on his sleeve. "The great Nathan Sahl, eh, Chief of Sovereign, wants to give me money. Tell me, old boy, does your money come from the living?"

"Careful, Drake, you know I'm not like Baylor –"

"What is it you want in return, oh Mighty One?"

"I need to speak with Evelyn, tonight."

Drake Owen's wife Evelyn was now the Foreign Secretary of the Kingdom Isle. She had worked hard to get there, having never taken a bribe, not even so much as a piece of stationery. This was Nathan's last hope of calling the whole thing off. If he could speak with her, she could plead his case. Maybe he could explain the crimes of his predecessor, Baylor, and that he was being set up by a secret society known as the Ministry of Men. He wondered whether Evelyn could strike a deal with Cat and the Union she represented; if anyone could it would be her, and the four of them could run away together, take refuge and start again.

"If you wish to speak to her, you will have to stand trial."

"I'll be dead before I even make it through the doors."

"You speak as if the war never ended."

"It didn't, we fight a war every day. With rations, riots and protests, smugglers and terrorists, our enemies abroad. We are on the edge of being a failing state, and I am the only thing holding it together."

Nathan took a drag on his cigar to mask his bitterness. Time had changed him; his position had made him a pessimist, paranoid, and who could blame him. The Kingdom was on the brink of collapse; the government was walking a tightrope. Abroad, the East and West were at war, the entire Union swept by the ideology of the Crane, and the only fragment of the free world left was the Kingdom Isle. Drake did heed his warning; they were like brothers, after all. Still, Nathan looked worn, they both did in a way, and it was hard to understand how it had ever come to this.

"I need to speak with Evelyn," said Nathan, for tomorrow took his mind again.

"You know that can't happen unless you're in a court of law."

"Do you really think I'm going to sit in front of those fools and let them try me as some sort of criminal? I only need to speak with her. What if she's in danger?" he went on. Nathan saw her as the only honourable soul left in the Old Abbey; a genuine friend surrounded by snakes. She would believe the truth about the Ministry's doings; she would remember the man, the friend Nathan was.

Drake stood; he couldn't sit there any longer with the stakes being so high. Nathan did the same.

"Eve's been in danger for a long time, but she's strong. She's the Foreign Secretary, Nathan, she knows what she's doing."

"You don't understand; the Council –"

"The Council? The *Union's* Council? Are you mad? Are you trying to get yourself hanged? Are you trying to start another war? You know what treason gets you." Drake was right to be frightened; the Council was a religion to the masses, bringing order to a foreign land, and the Union was a paradise compared to the hardships of Sovereign.

"I've seen the reserves, Drake; our food supplies won't last a year. Agreement with the Council ensures our survival. This country will go to ruin otherwise, and we need a way out."

"I have faith that we can turn things around – you need to work with the government, not against it. Stand trial, testify."

"Do you not think I've tried? The government can't help us, they don't decide a thing." Nathan stopped for a moment and thought about the Ministry of Men; he knew Drake wouldn't believe him even if he could tell him, but Evelyn might. "Our destinies don't end here. I can get you your money back, but I need to speak with her."

"Evelyn is all I have left in the world. She is good, she is kind, and she deserves much better than me." Drake's voice trembled as he fought off tears. "You've dug your own hole, Nathan, you knew what you were doing when you took the position, what it could do to your family."

"I'm not the man they say I am. You must know that; Evelyn must know that. Rose means more to me than anything else in the world."

Nathan didn't open up often, and Drake thought things over as the rain started to come down; he had always relied on Nathan to bring a sense of logic to a situation. Whenever there was a problem, Nathan had been the one to solve it, but now, where once there was trust, there was instability. Deep down Drake knew that Nathan had changed. Childhood seemed so far away; it was gone in the blink of an eye.

"I can't help you," said Drake, having finally found his courage. Saying no to one of the most powerful men in the world may have been the most courageous thing he had ever done.

"I suppose that's it?" Nathan replied.

"It is."

Drake calmly collected his coat and stood. He took a few steps forward and stubbed his cigar out on the floor before flicking it into a bin and walking away.

"I only wish you would let me help *you*," Nathan said, halting his friend as he crossed the garden path.

"Is it me who needs the help, or you?" asked Drake before walking away.

Nathan watched him go; there so much he wanted to say but he had no way to say it. Drake was right: the Union Council could not be trusted.

By the time Nathan summoned the strength to say another word, Drake was gone, and he was alone. Alone again and looking around as if to see if Cat was still watching.

Walking back much slower than before, he threw his cigar down on the perfect grass, where it smouldered. At the back door he remained as quiet as possible and went straight to his office for fear of waking Rose.

In his quiet space, Nathan sat down in his father's red leather chair in front of his long wooden desk. He set down the documents Cat had given him, his hand hovered over his letter opener for a moment and he caught a glimpse of a photograph. On his desk was a picture taken in Frist's restaurant ten years prior, when the four of them looked so young and full of hope. It was before the Ministry of Men and before the operations abroad. Nathan looked into their eyes and knew he was doing this for them. He pulled back the curtain, went into his pocket and withdrew the red rose, placing it on the windowsill so tomorrow would bring something new.

5

CONSEQUENCES

Drake took the path back past two scowling Kingdom Isle soldiers and went into the apartment lobby as worry melted his mind. He had come with money trouble and dreams of being saved by an old friend, but the heavy weight of the Union and the imminent collapse of his country was on his shoulders. He tried to breathe, tried to relax, and saw the limousine awaiting him on the other side. His elderly chauffeur, Arnold, leant on the car door with a kind smile, waiting for him.

"Evening, Arnold, thank you for waiting," said Drake.

"That's no problem, sir, the rain and the quiet round here has been peaceful, if you don't mind me saying." Arnold opened the door and Drake got in. The elderly chauffeur had become a close friend to Drake and Evelyn, having been their driver for years. Having led a simple life, he considered himself quite lucky. Arnold closed the door and headed over to the driver's side so they could begin their journey home.

"Is something bothering you, sir?" Arnold asked through the intercom, acknowledging the tell-tale frown on Drake's round face.

"No, Arnold, just another day," Drake replied, but the sweat on his brow spoke for itself.

Drake didn't talk to Arnold for the rest of the journey; he was over-analysing everything, unsure of what to do. There was no easy way out of this, everything had led to this moment; an awful guilt had overcome him, and hiding it away was taking its toll.

When Drake arrived home, he prayed Evelyn was in bed. Unable to go up, he made for the kitchen, took a tumbler from the cupboard and poured a harsh whiskey. Sitting and staring into nothing, he downed his drink; it was sharp and dry, reminding his throat of his demons, but it nowhere near brought the numbness he craved. Up again, he moved to the cupboard, rummaged behind the backboard, and found the bag of pills he had stashed long ago. He stared at the little white demons, remembering dilated pupils, the feeling of calm and the relaxation they brought, but also the deep sense of shame.

His fingers hovered over the bag. A tear rolled down his cheek; the spark had gone, and it wasn't worth losing her. Picking up the pills, his hand went to the bin whilst thoughts raced through his mind, some of want, some of self-pity. He took the bin bag to the front door, went down the steps to the street, and put it in the big bin for collection. Wiping his brow, he waited outside for a moment and obsessed as to whether this was the right thing to do. After a moment's contemplation he walked back up the steps and looked over his shoulder before going back inside, closing the door behind him. He wasn't tired at all and sat drinking the whole bottle dry until daybreak; only then did he collapse in bed stinking of regret.

The morning was bright and crisp, but Drake didn't see it; he slept through the alarms and Evelyn's pokes and shrugs. When she smelt the stale alcohol on his morning breath, she rolled out of bed in disgust. There was a growing divide between the gorgeous blue-eyed curly-haired brunette with her beautiful dark complexion, and the large plump aging average white male beside her. Evelyn put on her sharp blue business suit, went to two early-morning meetings, had brunch, gave an interview and a speech, and when she returned in the late afternoon it was only the way she slammed the door that woke him.

Drake stumbled down with a crushing headache, hobbling to the stairs, and there she stood, arms folded, back against the wall, looking down at the floor in disappointment. Drake often wondered how he had ended up with such an amazing woman and at such times worried that he didn't deserve her. He was always the victim of his own negative thinking: if nothing bad was going on around him he would see to it that it was, whereas in contrast Evelyn was a problem-solving optimist. She had worked so hard to become the Kingdom Foreign Secretary, but the burden was heavy, and heavier still with him.

It was growing harder to see the man in front of her for what he once was as their relationship became more strained. Drake's lifestyle had taken its toll, and though their relationship was at breaking point, under the surface she still loved him. Evelyn would not be where she was without him, and somewhere, under what he had become, was the man she fell in love with.

"Where have you been?" There was a sharp and unforgiving tone to her question.

"I had some business to attend to with a client," he replied, a shallow, transparent lie.

"It's four in the afternoon, Drake, I can't do this anymore."

Drake stumbled down the stairs in his vest and pyjamas, his hair rough and his eyes tired. Everything he thought of saying he had said before and it had worked on a few occasions – but not this time. Evelyn found it harder to believe him these days, although in the past it had been easier than wasting her time with worry.

"I'm sorry, it won't happen again. I –"

"I hope it went okay," she said, remembering his struggle with himself and his business affairs. She did not want to go into detail, all she wanted was for him to be better, to go back to being the man she used to know.

"Maybe we can go for dinner, or I can cook or something? Here, I'll make Bolognese."

Drake darted off down the hallway to the kitchen so

quickly that Evelyn could barely keep up. Her phone began to sound. Upon entering the kitchen, she found Drake already banging through pots and pans and rummaging for ingredients in an incoherent and sadly humorous fashion.

"Drake," she said, but amidst the clattering he could not hear her. "*Drake*," she said again, to no avail. "*Drake!*"

Drake turned and saw her anger. "The Prime Minister has called a cabinet assembly; I have to go."

Drake paused, speechless, and dropped a pan onto the counter and the rest went with it. Again the conversation he had had with Nathan played in his mind, about Evelyn being in danger, about the Union, about the so-called Ministry of Men. "You have a meeting?" he asked with uncertainty in his voice. Evelyn sighed; she had told him more than once and worried about that cluttered brain of his.

"It's about Nathan, he hasn't attended since taking Baylor's place. People have gone missing; the community control sector won't communicate with us – he needs to answer for everything."

Drake was torn. On the one hand, his love, and on the other, his best friend. For too long he had denied the rumours about Nathan. He was afraid to admit them, afraid to accept they could be true, but denial only went so far when the brightness in Evelyn's blue eyes turned to fear.

"Do you really think he's done these things?" he asked.

"I wish it wasn't so."

"Maybe he was set up by the Ministry of Men, by his predecessor. Maybe he wants to fix things."

"Drake, I know this is hard for you, but the Ministry of Men doesn't exist. Experiments, torture, they *do* exist. Even if it was Baylor, Nathan was second in command."

"How can you be sure?" asked Drake with a sense of pride and denial, unable to accept such things about his best friend.

"Open your eyes, Drake." Evelyn was frustrated and beyond exhausted; she loved Rose and had once loved Nathan like a brother.

Drake wasn't taking it well, he was beyond tired too, and he banged his fist upon the kitchen counter. "My eyes are open!" he shouted, before regretting his reaction. Evelyn backed away, all too familiar with his erratic nature. It had brought a tear to her eye, which she tried to hide. "I'm sorry. I –"

"I've seen the facts, the figures, the interrogations, the brutality first hand," she said as Drake began to cower. "Has something happened?"

"What do you mean?"

"You've been acting strange all morning, is something wrong? Are you using again?"

"No," he said with deep remorse, looking down to hide his guilt. Right now, Drake wished he was, for it would be easier to fix than deal with the bankruptcy. He looked pale and even though he wasn't using, his betrayal in seeing Nathan was enough to make him feel guilty.

"Are you sure?"

"I feel like we should just get out of here," he said, to her surprise.

Evelyn looked at him and almost laughed, despite the sadness of the whole situation. "And go where? There's nowhere to go and I have a sinking ship to run." She folded her arms and moved away. A part of her wanted to hug him, to make up, but she couldn't right now, not today.

A knock on the door interrupted them; Arnold was outside. Drake tried to kiss Evelyn, but she turned as he met her cheek.

"Goodbye, Drake."

"Goodbye –"

There were many more things that he wanted to say, but she disappeared down the corridor and he was left hanging. Evelyn had gone as quickly as she had appeared, down the steps to where Arnold waited.

"Good morning," she said, taken aback by Arnold's expression. He seemed less cheery than usual; everyone was acting strangely today.

"Good morning, Mrs. Owen, let me take that bag for you."

"Arnold, you say that every day, and every day I say I'll carry it myself. I admire your politeness and thank you for it, but I assure you I'm quite capable."

"Sorry, I guess it's a generation thing."

She headed down the steps towards the limousine and took her seat, then the doors closed, sealing the heavily armoured vehicle and shielding her from the world. It was safe and pristine, a glorious ride, but she would never grow accustomed to it. All Evelyn wanted to do was walk to work as if everything was normal, like she had ten years ago, but that was just a dream.

"How's things today? You look concerned – trouble at home?" Evelyn asked. She noticed that Arnold was rather quiet, and she missed the way her friendly old driver told tales of times long past.

"I haven't been too well of late," he replied. The car rolled slowly down the gated road; it wasn't worth speeding up because of the several roadblocks ahead of them as they made their way through dark, dirty streets. Near Sovereign's centre, Evelyn heard the unrest through the reinforced glass. Arnold's driving was a little off this morning, although Evelyn barely noticed until he took an unexpected turn down Fifth.

"You're going the wrong way," she said through the intercom.

"There's a garbage truck on fire, darn protesters again, so we have to take a detour."

A detour was not such a good idea. It meant heading straight down Capital Street, towards the Gold Road – once the fastest way to get to the Great Houses and the Old Abbey, although for the past few years it had been blocked off to most, and for good reason. It wasn't long before they saw rioters and protestors swarming over streets once paved with gold. Trash splatted against the sides of the car and debris bounced off chipping paint. Crowds clashed against riot shields and men were arrested, never to be seen again. Evelyn put on a brave face – it was chilling and forced a sad guilt upon her; she wasn't numb to it like most politicians, she truly cared. Having risen from a working-class background, the people's suffering was always on her mind. She wanted to help them, but it seemed impossible now, as riot shields guarded either side of the vehicle against a sea of protest with a powerful tide.

Despite the uproar, they passed through the golden gates and rolled at a slow speed towards the Great Houses and the Old Abbey. Now the once luxurious gardens were filled with protestors, and the fences had retreated, now topped with barbed wire. The buildings, once bright stone, were dark and crooked, and maintenance had given up repairing the many broken windows. It was a testament to how the mighty had fallen over ten long years.

Evelyn scrabbled all her paperwork together as Arnold opened the door, and she exited with her travel case and documents in hand. "Thank you," she said, ready to make her way inside.

"Excuse me, Mrs. Owen!" Arnold shouted above the noise of protest surrounding them, and Evelyn stopped in her tracks. "You forgot one of your letters."

In his hand was a red Union envelope she didn't recognise. The crimson colour made the world pause as she stared at the embossed insignia of the crimson flying crane. For a moment there was nothing, just her and the letter, and then a brick soared through the air, bouncing off the limousine and startling her back to reality. Arnold put one arm around her and turned to find the culprit, but there were a thousand vicious shouting faces in front of them.

"Come on, you have to get inside," he said as Evelyn was once again lost for a moment. She would have remembered such a letter ... It must have come this morning, but her thoughts of Drake and everything else had clouded her judgement.

"Don't tell anyone that I almost forgot this, Arnold."

"Who have I got to tell, Evie? I promise."

"I suppose I'd best be going," she said with a polite nod.

"Unless you want another brick ... Have a good day," said Arnold, this time with a nervous smile, before getting back in the limousine.

Evelyn turned to the mob one last time, knowing the culprit could have killed her and knowing that might have been a kind of justice. Pushed to the edge by a lack of food rations, the collapse of education, welfare and healthcare, the people were not the ones to blame. Though most politicians believed the mob's actions to be brutal, Evelyn knew that they were a cry for help, not a cry for war. After some internal contemplation, she walked along the side of the Old Abbey to the adjoining Great Houses. Ancient buildings of grand stone marked by time, wisdom and greatness, the architecture boasted of early democracy's finest achievements, rebuilt over time and outliving the great artists who had added to their vibrancy over the years.

At the top of the huge stone stairs, Evelyn was met with grand wooden doors held open by two old honour guards. The walls and the doors told the story of the history of the Sovereign kings with murals and tapestries. Inside, what were once fresh oak and forest-green halls were covered in dust. Most of the buildings were derelict now, and public visits were no longer permitted. It had become a place of high fences and riot shields. Evelyn took the hidden spiral staircase just off the main hallway, but even then she was late. It was almost seven and the cathedral bells would ring soon. The short-cut led to an old room, green and oak again, with red leather furniture, and smoky from the fireplace that kept the cabinet members warm. Inside were several uninterested faces, for a deep sense of apathy shrouded everyone and everything present. Nothing was as bright and grand as it used to be; the country and its leaders had lost their shine – all apart from her.

Sitting around the large oval cabinet table were once ambitious and hopeful leaders who still tried their best to hold things together. One was Prime Minister Davies, a good man in truth, the best of a bad bunch. Bold, charismatic and relatively youthful despite his silver hair, Davies was strong, having taken responsibility and earned respect at a time of crisis when no one else could take the burden. He knew what he would face when he first took the oath to serve, after the previous Prime Minister had died in a rather suspicious gardening accident.

Evelyn entered late, mid speech. She took the seat nearest the door, as her seat by the fire was taken. No one seemed to take note of her, and she noticed that none of them looked well, Davies seeming the worst. Bearing the whole nation's problems on his shoulders had aged him, and yet this was when he was at his best. He stood at the end of the great table, feet apart, his fists pressed into leather over oak; his knuckles pressed into the woodwork where the dents from hundreds of leaders who had stood here before him had also made their mark.

"*The media has broken me; these very houses have broken me*," he said in his cool crisp voice.

"Prime Minister, let us have order," Minister Miles pleaded, a large old man with a high voice, attempting to bring a sense of calm.

"What do you suggest I do? The North is soon to starve, and it won't be long before the mob outside comes through the gates. It's bad enough having the community control officers on our streets; even the gates won't hold them forever."

Davies clearly felt hopeless, and even Evelyn didn't say anything to interrupt him. Her family lived in the Northern Quadrant, an area hidden from the media but hit hard by the economic standstill. It was rampant with poverty, poor education, danger and deceit. Even she had been denied the right to travel there anymore. Her ties to Nathan had also brought mistrust; no member of the cabinet would say it aloud, but it was obvious to her and it made her hate him even more.

Davis stood and leaned on the desk, his hands in his pockets. He looked out of the window at the protesting crowds and the riot control officers below, his back to his ministers. His entire cabinet sat in silence. "Look at all these people, what do you suppose I should do?" he asked.

"There isn't really anything we can do; Nathan has refused our offer of a trial. We are here more as prisoners than leaders; his people are watching us, mocking us," said Miles. Miles was at heart a member of the Ministry of Men and his role was to say such things in order to make them true.

"We could have him killed?" suggested Ms. Barnes, who was also a member of the Ministry of Men, but neither her nor Miles knew of each other's allegiance to the Ministry.

"We'd be no better than him. No, no, he must testify. This is a democracy." Davies's voice echoed through the office, as it always did, but it had a new-found habit of failing to resonate into action.

"Why don't we bring him in? Let's not wait for him to come to us any longer, we have given him enough time." Miles spoke in a slow and uncertain way, as if he were being overly careful over every word.

Everyone looked at him in silent approval, except Davies, who stared out of the window, his face unsurprised, a sense of unwillingness shrouding him.

"And who will bring him? His community control officers? The man has a small army at his gates," said Ms. Hayworth.

Minister Miles gulped and his heart almost beat through his chest – it was hard to tell whether it was his age, obesity, or the four coffees he'd drunk this morning. Davies's posture changed. With no more left to give he turned around to face the room.

"When did we ever think it would come to this, eh? I've failed."

Davies hadn't felt well for quite some time. The whole point of his career had been to make things better, but the system was inherently flawed, and his position had not made a difference. "Do we have anyone who can bring him in?"

"The royal guard," replied Miles as he stood and walked over to Evelyn. He picked up her pile of documents and put them down on Davies's desk.

Davies knew the royal guard were more a symbol than a force. They were old … but might just do the job. He opened his drawer and retrieved his favourite pen along with his notepad.

"This is a warrant for Nathan's arrest; you don't have to sign this, only I do. You don't have to share my burden."

No one dared say a word; they had all been pushed too far and seen the photographs Miles had provided in secrecy. They had all seen the suffering, and it meant they had no choice. Each of them was aware that a signature could sign their own fate, but it didn't matter now.

In silence it was passed around the table and signed by each member; not one of them hesitated. Not even Evelyn: she thought of the man Nathan had become, not the one Rose thought he was.

"There is a letter here with the Crane stamp of the Union Council," said Miles. The room was silent, and Miles passed it to Davies, feeling the dreaded insignia of the Crane against his fingertips.

"This is from the Union Council, a Signature of Assistance." Davies knew that such a letter was a move of forced assistance, of *intervention*. Formal acceptance of Union aid, *peace-bringing,* meant the death of democracy.

"We can't," said Evelyn, breaking her silence.

"It's good of you to say something, Mrs. Owen, no matter how obvious," Davies joked.

"I'm quite surprised you signed the first document, given your history," said Ms. Hayworth, bitterly adding to the sting Davies had given. There were bickers and cheers from the other members, but nothing more.

"You know I hate him more than anyone here."

"Forgive Ms. Hayworth, Mrs. Owen," said Miles, trying to end the conflict in haste; the last thing they needed was to be divided.

"I will take pleasure in tearing up this letter, or wiping my arse with it," joked Davies with an enigmatic smile before pouring himself a glass of water. Everybody in the room looked on, less willing to boast for fear of prying Union ears. "A toast, for today is bad, but I hope tomorrow will be better. God, I wish this was something stronger."

Davies placed down his glass, picked up the envelope and moved towards the heat of the fire. There he stared at the haunting insignia; in the flame it appeared more red. He went to tear the letter in two, but the bellowing vibrations of the nearby cathedral clock shook the room as the clock struck seven, and Davies hesitated. Everyone was on edge for a moment, before beginning to chuckle, all except Evelyn. Davies shrugged, wiped his brow and threw the envelope into the flames with a certain smugness. The letter rested for a moment; its edges crinkled. It started to spark, and *BOOM*, the room became an inferno, an explosion shattering everyone and everything, vaporising them too quickly for anyone to scream.

Smoke billowed as the Great Houses burned to the ground; large crowds surged outside the gates, slowing the entry of the emergency services. No survivors were reported on the news as the country went into a state of emergency. The government was no more, and no political party would be strong enough to stand.

The only security would be martial law – but that would come after the riots, after a night of mayhem. Tonight, there would be anarchy, robbery; tomorrow, swift order. At the eleventh hour, the Union had delivered what they had promised, but Nathan Sahl knew not the cost. Watching the explosion and the Great Houses erupting into flames, he stood in his armour upon the rooftop, unable to believe what he was seeing. Under strict instructions from the Union and in fear of their repercussions, he waited for midnight as the people below celebrated. Fireworks filled the sky, alarms rang in the streets and chaos ensued as the people danced, for democracy was dead.

6

THE RED NIGHT

Sovereign erupted into chaos. The city was ransacked, community control officers were fought off with petrol bombs, bricks, and courage. The Kingdom's small army hadn't yet been deployed and hired guns guarded the gates of the few, firing shots at the many. Amidst the chaos Nathan Sahl stood upon his rooftop with a heavy hand on his heart. He donned his black armoured vest; it was etched with swirls and flowers over a white battle-armour shirt. A heavy overcoat flowed over his shoulders and down towards his combat trousers and light military boots.

Call after call came through from Kingdom forces at the scene asking for confirmation, and though Nathan answered each one, his mind was elsewhere. Evelyn had taken over his thoughts, and though Nathan didn't shed a tear or curse the Union, he felt the weight of his decision. He was afraid of what the Union Council could do, and he obsessed over making any wrong move, as they were his only hope. He said a short prayer for

Evelyn. Facing Rose or, God forbid, Drake might be the hardest things he would ever have to do, but he had to be strong for Rose and their child.

Hours passed as he listened to the screams, smelt the smoke and forced himself to watch as the Great Houses burned to the ground. It seemed so surreal. The noise and chaos of it all augmented the constant sounds in his mind: the past few weeks of tension; his election; the demands of the Ministry and his government.

Nathan wondered how he would go down in history: as the great betrayer, or the saviour of his people. He tried to hide his core insecurity about being a coward, about being the only man in Sovereign history to let the Union in. Holding the letter in his free hand, he felt foolish thinking even for a moment that the Union might fail. Until today the threat of imminent betrayal had been everywhere, but as he read Councillor Rogan's letter everything became clear:

At the seventh cathedral bell, enemies will burn. Let Sovereign consume itself in anarchy, let it bleed and run with blood to disguise the red night to come. No government means martial law and your power as Chief of Defence will be infallible. When the eleventh sounds my soldiers will land and at the twelfth let us cleanse the Ministry of Men once and for all.

Nathan took his hand from his chest to reveal the insignia of the Union Crane that he had been hiding. His new armour was a gift from Rogan, and it brought him no pride to wear it. His Sovereign armour, which had served him for years, remained locked away in his study; the new replica would have to do.

Nathan withdrew his lighter from his pocket and watched the letter wither into nothing. He was anxious, both eager and afraid of what he had started. It was easy to wish it didn't have to be this way, it was easy to think there was something else he could have done, but the Ministry was closing in, the government was closing in – he had had no choice. Nathan knew something bad was going to happen, but nothing had prepared him for the full extent of what he had agreed to. Arguing back and forth with himself, the call finally came to interrupt him, and he clicked his earpiece as the flames of the fire reflected in his dark brown eyes.

"Nathan, this is Chief Councillor Rogan," said the voice, but Nathan could not reply straightaway; he was lost for words, unsure of what to say to the soft cold calm voice on the other end, so free of trouble. "Nathan, my son, do you hear me?"

"I do," he replied after much hesitation, "good evening, Councillor."

"The Great Houses burn along with their outdated ideas. Now is your time, the Council welcomes you."

Nathan remained reserved and hesitant, having done what was asked despite his guilt. He knew the Council's game and the danger they presented, and he thought of Evelyn, and those who would follow. There was no going back.

"I aim to serve, my Council," he said, although it pained him to say it.

"As we expected, but there is much more to accomplish. Our troops are prepared; give your word and they go house to house to dispose of the Ministry of Men."

"Thank you, Councillor, our action will be swift, I give my word."

"Our enemies will die tonight, but there is still a debt to be paid: the Titan."

"Understood," Nathan replied. He remembered the Titan, the huge flying machine long lain dormant at the East airfield. In his youth he had marvelled as it towered high above him. He had wished to see it fly, but if only he knew the cost. With the government calling for his tribunal, he had barely had time to think about it, but knew that his close associate Monroe would be losing sleep over it.

"I have no doubt that you will return the Titan, but there is one more thing … You must leave no stone unturned. Prove yourself: you must kill the confession."

It took a moment for Nathan to understand what Rogan meant. *Kill the confession,* he thought. Then he remembered: it could only mean one thing and he wished it wasn't so. He wondered how Rogan would have come to know such a thing, but it was easy to assume his spies were everywhere. "Understood, my Council."

"Farewell," said Rogan, and then he was gone. His call left Nathan alone again fearing the consequences; there was no going back. Behind him was a bitter and broken Sovereign, one he had betrayed, and the only way forward was the Union.

～

A large yellow moon lit the clear sky and beamed down through the bombed-out church upon Sovereign's hillside. Through aged stone walls, under the open sky was a priest, almost as wise as he was old. He spent his time in the church and never left, living off donations, sleeping in the shelter of the pulpit under his God's watchful eyes despite frost, rain, wind or shine. His sight was poor, but his hearing was better. White, thinning hair, dark eyes and a heavy, ragged cloak that doubled as a blanket on cold nights shimmered in the darkness. The priest was unsettled by a dark feeling in the air tonight. He prayed for hours, meditated, until the rumble of a large engine on loose stone shook the walls.

The ignition was cut, and boots hit the ground. Men stood in the distance; they talked and laughed, but one split off from the rest. With each crunch two boots came closer and the priest knew who was coming. A dark and damaged figure, one all too familiar – he could feel them all watching him from the overgrown entryway.

"Is that you?" called the priest into the darkness.

"It is I, Father."

The priest didn't show any sign of happiness, nostalgia or remembrance at the sound of the man's voice – he showed no sign of welcome.

"The nameless confessor," he said in a solemn tone. "I had a dream yesterday; I heard your voice in a violent wind."

"Spare me your visions, priest."

The man staring back at the priest was a different

man in the darkness. Nathan Sahl had prepared himself for war. He stood tall in his new armour covered by his long overcoat, his shoulders wide and square and his hands at his front. On his chest, the symbol of the Union's Crane burnt into his being. Here was a different man, far from his family and friends. A man who used to seek blessing before war.

Nathan stared at the old man with his chin held high, knowing the priest would never know his name. Even Nathan needed someone to share his burdens with, share his fears and dark thoughts without risk or shame. A name meant a face, and a face meant it was all too real. If the priest had seen him, he would have told Nathan to leave his pistol before entering the church, but he had not and could not.

"Have you come to ask for forgiveness?"

"Maybe I've come for forgiveness, maybe I've come for confession."

"For five years you have sought my advice, and never have you shared your name."

"And?"

"Maybe it is time to confess even that," said the wise old priest.

Nathan looked around the bombed-out church. The priest stood barefoot on the hard floor; it was cold and the chill within these walls was something Nathan could never get used to. He leant on an old pillar and folded his arms, not ready for what he had to do. The priest stared in his direction, waiting for him to speak, but Nathan was quiet; in truth he feared the wrath of God, even though his new Union allies had done away with such beliefs and now idolised their prophet Elias Crane. The wicked faith of Unionism was not something Nathan wanted to adopt. He was at heart a believer in the dark and the light, the old way, the way of Kings. The priest made it all so easy to believe: he had premonitions and dreams that no science could explain.

"Has something got your tongue? I sense fear in you; how many more have you killed?"

Nathan thought of Evelyn first. He could see her now in her wedding dress as he stood there as the best man. "Not enough," he said in an attempt to hide his sorrow.

"How many have you left without parents?"

"Many."

"How many have you left without children?" The priest did not wish to hear an answer to that question and shook his head.

"You know not the horrors of war, the price I have paid and the burden upon my shoulders. You sat within the safety of these walls whilst I bled for our country. There wasn't a second when I had the right to choose, when I had had the right to decide."

"All men get to choose; good men often choose the hardest path where the worst of us choose the easiest."

"I don't have time for your lessons, priest."

"I pray to God, and do you know what the Almighty tells me?"

"What?"

"God has stopped listening to you. He has given enough to you. There are horrors coming your way and prayer alone will not stop them."

His words struck fear into Nathan's heart, but he tried to be brave, hide the pain for Rose, for his soon-to-be-born son. It would take more than that to scare him, but the priest was testing his patience and now was not the time; it was not the reason he was here.

"Confess all you like but I will not ask for reconciliation. God forgives the worst of sins, but not yours – you must ask him yourself."

Nathan stepped towards the priest clenching his fist, his leather glove crinkled tight. Looking down, he saw a frail man who knew too much and saw too little, but he was a kind man, and a role model. One of the few people Nathan had ever looked up to, one of the few from whom he'd sought advice. He remembered the first day he came here, after military service. The priest was the only man who had ever seen him cry. Nathan had carried him, fed him, read his sermons and even sung. He wiped a tear from his eye.

"I didn't come here for your forgiveness or your council," he said with a chilling calmness as the priest turned away and shook his head in disapproval.

"You seem more guilty now than ever."

"I never asked for this. I don't want those I love to see what I have become."

The priest heard well enough the sorrowful desperation in Nathan's voice, and in his visions he had seen why Nathan was here tonight. Scrambling upright with the aid of his walking stick, his hollow frame creaked beneath him as he stumbled towards Nathan. Too weak and feeble to stand, Nathan caught him before he fell.

"I know what you have come here to do, I have

always known the price of listening to your sins, and I am ready, Nathan," said the priest, his glazed blind eyes offering acceptance. If the priest could have seen Nathan's, he would have seen fear, regret and love for a man who had loved him more than his own father. Nathan was lost for words, for the priest knew, he always knew – but it was too late. He wrapped his hand tight around his neck and squeezed. The priest's eyes remained open, staring into Nathan's soul as he gasped for life itself.

"Forgive me," Nathan whispered, unable to look away as the priest choked and whispered something softly into his ear whilst fading from the tight grasp around his neck.

"I forgive you," he said, and the words echoed around Nathan's mind as he, a man trying so desperately to act without conscience, felt the weight of his decision. His grip still tight, the priest grew lifeless. He laid down the body gently, with respect, and tore a large crimson curtain from the altar, placing it over his head. He stood for a moment staring down at the lifeless priest, a man he had respected but a man who could not live.

There is no going back, he told himself. Whatever Rogan wanted, whatever his Union, his Council wanted, they would get. If it meant paradise for him and Rose, a life away from this rotting island, it would be worth it. That was how he tried to justify his actions while resting his head in his hands alongside the fallen priest.

"From the light to the earth we pass from birth. From

beginning to end, we return what it's worth. God take this candle burnt out bright, take him from the darkness and walk him to the light."

Nathan said the old words and placed a hand on the priest's chest before struggling to his feet and turning around; he didn't dare look back. The world seemed to spin as he made his way outside and through the over-grown garden. He stopped himself just before the gate and had to hold on; it was hard to accept the sacrifices for his family, and those he would continue to give. Nathan took a deep breath and assumed a strong and imposing posture, before marching across the stones to greet his soldiers.

The laughter of the men outside the vehicle fell silent on his arrival. Four of the men scattered and entered the back of the truck; only one remained. He turned to face Nathan without any warm welcome. His name was Caleb Walker, a rough-cut soldier, with fierce eyes and a scar under his chin. His hair was buzzed back. He was a loud-mouthed special operations mili-tary veteran. He wasn't tall but was broad and agile; years of training and proven loyalty made him the perfect right-hand man.

"I get what needs to be done, but are you sure you want to do this yourself?" Caleb asked – a brave ques-tion that no other man would have dared to utter. They were brothers in arms, having served together many times before.

"There is no other choice, my friend," Nathan replied, patting him on the shoulder.

"How many tonight?"

"All of them," said Nathan. Caleb raised an eyebrow in surprise, then grinned and spat his gum onto the floor before walking briskly to the driver's side in excitement. Climbing in, Caleb banged his fist against the glass, forcing those in the back into silence. The truck started and they sped off into the night. The priest took Nathan's mind, as did Drake, waiting for Evelyn to come home. He sank back into his seat hating every minute of tonight but knowing there was no other way.

He listened in on his headset to reports of what was happening in the centre of Sovereign. The public were lawless, riots had gone on throughout the day and into the night. Kingdom Isle soldiers had been instructed not to intervene, at least not until things were at their worst. In the background documents were signed and culprits dealt with as the fire gave the Union and therefore Nathan the cover he needed. Blame for the fire was placed on members of the Ministry of Men: oligarchs, bureaucrats, lawyers, Kingdom's military generals, who hadn't the faintest clue that the Union, or Nathan would strike. Nathan didn't know what the Union would do but they had promised to cleanse the Kingdom of his enemies. When the call came, he felt ashamed for his loss; Evelyn was gone, and he didn't have time to ask himself how he would live with it.

He pulled a piece of paper from his pocket revealing a list of every member of the Ministry of Men, provided by Councillor Rogan. Nathan circled twenty names of former friends, now enemies; they would all pay the price tonight.

Like clockwork the Union plan clicked into place.

At eleven, Union soldiers crossed the stormy Channel with no resistance. In exchange for relinquishing their vows, Kingdom military officers were given extended rights as Union Front soldiers, with the promise of being able to join their chief aboard the Titan. The gold insignia of the Sovereign crown was replaced by the red Union Crane, and all the soldiers had to do was adopt their new uniform and obey their commands; then they could live new lives with their families in the utopia that was the Union.

"I get what needs to be done but are you sure you want to do this one yourself?" asked Caleb once again whilst driving at speed down a bumpy country road.

"I have to see him, out of respect," Nathan replied.

"I get it, I do, but the past is the past. I can do it, or have one of the boys in the back do it."

"Some things don't stay buried unless you put them in the ground yourself," said Nathan, and Caleb shrugged before taking out another piece of chewing gum and putting it in his mouth. He wasn't one for such smart lessons; Caleb was a soldier not a poet. He just wanted action. He didn't care who he was fighting, or why, he just wanted a good fight. It had been years since they had been alongside each other; when Nathan went into politics, Caleb went into private security abroad, but when he was called back, he came immediately.

Caleb had no knowledge of politics of it all, they didn't interest him, but Nathan's warning invoked a forgotten grudge. He had waited a long time for what was coming, and his thoughts of killing the privileged few took away the dark calm beauty of the outskirts of Sovereign.

The truck stormed down winding country roads over potholes beyond repair. The journey wasn't long, but Nathan watched the clock, counting every minute. Far from the outskirts of the city, where miles of working farms were abandoned because of poisoned soil and robbery, lay the grand estates of the highest Ministry members. Only a handful of people still held onto such grand estates in the Kingdom; most had been laid waste, with no water or fuel, but this one was well stocked.

Crashing through the gates of a huge country house a few miles outside Sovereign, boots stomped on the stony ground and ten soldiers entered the building. Guns at the ready, balaclavas on, they smashed the door down as Nathan and Caleb watched from the truck. They had forgotten the losses that had gone before; this was the first kill that felt just.

The soldiers swept through the downstairs of the house. Happy family photos filled the corridors along with the medals and ornaments of a decorated Sovereign veteran. Commander Carl Jacobs and his wife Debbie Jacobs were enjoying a bottle of red wine in the living room when the soldiers entered. Carl was carving a wooden sculpture and Debbie was reading a newspaper. The soldiers booted through the door, guns high, screaming orders. Jacobs dropped the sculpture and stood in shock. Debbie screamed before dropping her glass of wine, which shattered on the floor and ran red all over the carpet.

"No sudden moves, Commander!" shouted an officer, and for the first time in his life Jacobs didn't know what to do. Caught at home without protection, unarmed and surrounded, he wondered for a moment who would have the nerve. The great fire had not yet hit the news, and nor had the rioting, since Nathan had signed a gagging order to keep everything quiet until tomorrow.

"You're making a mistake, kid … What's the meaning of this? Don't you know who I am? Lower your weapons, immediately!" shouted Jacobs as he stared at their Union uniforms in disbelief.

"We can't do that, Commander, we have our orders," said the officer, who until today would have gone in fear of such a man.

Debbie put up no fight as the soldiers took hold of her, but their harsh handling made Jacobs resist. More soldiers moved in, and the officer cracked Jacobs's jaw with his pistol; the taste of blood let him know they weren't messing.

"Don't do this," Jacobs instructed, still reluctant to beg through a split lip; but he and his wife were zip-tied, gagged and bags were placed over their heads before he could say any more.

Unable to breathe, he worried for Debbie's life more than his own as memories of his training kicked in. The soldiers dragged him outside and into the middle of the courtyard, his knees grazing on the cold bare stone. Debbie sobbed, muffled by the bag, but Jacobs didn't say anything. The bags on their heads were removed, and blinding fog-lights shone down from the truck.

More soldiers looked on as they took off the prisoners' gags.

"Spare my wife, spare Debbie. That's all I want."

"The Great Houses burn, you and your Ministry of terrorists are to blame, and Chief Sahl has allied us with the Union to bring order and justice –"

The officer's short speech was interrupted by Carl's laughter. As tragic as the situation was, in his final moments he could not help but laugh at the shit he was being fed.

"To blame? You really are a wet wipe stained with horse-shit, aren't you, soldier. This is madness, where is he? Where is that cowardly bastard?"

The sound of boots crushing stones on the ground came from behind the truck, and then Nathan was in plain sight. His presence brought silence to all.

"You can whine all you like, Commander," he said whilst puffing on a cigarette. The smoke misted around him in the truck's fog-lights as the others stared on in silence. The officer was quick to fall into line and moved to the side, close to Jacobs, afraid to break the tension.

"You don't have to do this; we can give you whatever you want," Jacobs pleaded, looking up at Nathan, having spent so much time looking down at him during his career. Jacobs was apprehensive but believed he would live, having talked his way out of worse situations. Then a young soldier burst from the house carrying a crumpled piece of paper, and a part of Jacobs sank.

"Sir, you need to see this," he said to Nathan. Approaching, he passed Nathan a letter, and Nathan cast a glance as Jacobs and the commander swallowed his pride.

"A letter from the Prime Minister urging you to take action against me, signed by fellow Ministry members." Nathan's expression changed to one of anger. It was true, it was all true. He had proof, he wasn't paranoid or deluded, they *were* working together to take him down. "You fool, what was the point in replacing Baylor just to kill me? I wasn't him; I wasn't the same!"

"But that's the point, isn't it, Nathan. We needed someone who would continue the torture, the arrests, the crushing of civil liberties. It became abundantly clear when you knew the full depth of Baylor's actions that you weren't the man for the job."

Nathan scrunched up the piece of paper and dropped it on the floor. "How long did I have before you were going to take me out?" There was rage in his eyes, for Nathan had given everything for the Ministry for ten long years. On every military mission for them, he had seen good men die – and for what?

"Not soon enough."

"You left me no choice; it was all of you, or me."

"Do you really believe you can trust the Union? They will kill you the first chance they get; imagine if your father could see you now, a Unionist!"

"You dare bring him into this!" said Nathan with a bitter change of tone; he hated any mention of his father: the alcoholism, the beatings, his post-traumatic stress.

"He was famous for firing on his own men, and the same sickness will come to you."

"Enough!" Nathan shouted, taking a few steps back, his temper quick to rise. He waited for a moment, thinking about what to do, how to end this, and in that moment Jacobs hopped to his feet. No one had noticed him tearing through the zip-ties with his pocket-knife in the shadows; this was his moment. He slashed at the officer's throat, pulled him close, took his gun and used him for cover. The soldier gargled, unable talk, spitting blood as the rest of them crowded Nathan to protect him. Jacobs emptied the pistol and each of the soldiers fell to the ground. He turned to Debbie; she lay, close to lifeless, on the floor in a puddle of blood, caught in the crossfire.

"Debbie!" he cried, pulling off the mask to check her pulse – it was weak. He fell to his knees alongside her, holding her close as she took her last breaths. He didn't often show emotion, but this broke him.

Nathan was only winded; he pulled himself to his feet. The bulletproof vest had done its job, but he still felt the pain. He limped towards the truck. Jacobs almost didn't see him stand amidst his loss; he turned to fire and pulled the trigger with red and vengeful eyes, but there was no ammunition.

"Coward!" shouted Jacobs, too weak to give pursuit as Nathan scrambled towards the truck and into the safety of its cabin.

The officer lay in pain on the ground nearby, and Jacobs turned to him with a sickening anger, a fury he had left on the battlefield long ago newly awoken. He rolled over and on top of him, and the officer's fearful eyes stared back. Fist after fist rained down as he bludgeoned the soldier's face. Blow by blow he was beaten to death.

Knuckles bloody, bruised and broken, his eyes wide and heart beating fast, Jacobs heard the truck's engine start. Desperate to get to his feet, he fell back onto his knees, blood on his hands, clutching his stomach as blood poured out. The adrenaline began to wear off and he felt the full brunt of the stinging wound as the truck sped into the distance. Breathing heavily, he held out his bloody hand in the vehicle's direction, then he gave up hope and wiped a tear from his eye. Searching the officer's corpse, he pulled a document from his top left pocket.

At 01:00 hours, Saturday 5th January 2095, the Kingdom government was destroyed in a coup planned by terrorist leaders of the Central army. As Chief of Defence, I have made the decision to ally with the Union Front in contract and honour, to rid this state of the perpetrators and cleanse our homeland. Those who join us will be rewarded as Union soldiers, those who do not will answer for their crimes as terrorists.

Commander Jacobs had read enough; he scrunched up the piece of paper covered in blood and tossed it aside.

Searching the officer's body, he found a phone. Attempting to unlock it, his bloody hands shook and slipped. He desperately entered a number. *Ring-ring, ring-ring … You have reached the voicemail of …* He hung up the call and redialled as fast as he could, hiding his tears and agony as the truck roared in the distance. The phone rang and this time someone answered.

"Dad, it's two in the morning," came the voice of a tough, purple-haired young woman on the other side of Sovereign, tired and half asleep.

"I'm so happy to hear your voice, Lydia. I'm so happy you –" He trembled, weak and breathless, unsure of what to say. There were so many things, so many he would not have the time to say again.

"What's wrong, Dad, what's happened?"

"I'm sorry, kiddo, I'm sorry, I didn't see this coming; I love you."

"You're scaring me, you aren't making any sense." Lydia's tiredness had turned to concern as Carl looked at Debbie one last time. Then he looked up to the night sky, oblivious to the roaring engine in the distance.

"They will come for you too, you need to –"

"Who's coming? Please tell me what's wrong, please!"

"Get out, just get out. The Great Houses, the Union, Nathan Sahl."

"No, I –" Her tone switched now from fear to concentration as her father tried to hide his pain. His voice was faint, with a sadness she had never heard before, but he tried to stay strong for her as the sound of the truck grew closer.

"We've been betrayed, kid. Nathan is to blame for all this …"

She was full of sorrow and a sick sense of worry; nothing could have prepared her for this.

"Your suit, where is it?"

"It's here."

"Well, put it on, do what you do best. Remember I

love you and your mother loves you. Goodbye kiddo, we have to say goodbye." Despite the pain, Jacobs smiled to feel this one last ray of warmth from the love they shared.

"I love you too, Dad. And I will, I promise." The sound of an engine, and crackling, preceded the end of the call, as the truck mowed them down at speed. Jacobs lay on the cold gravel looking up at the stars and still holding his wife's hand. He closed his eyes as he took his final breath lying next to her.

Cold and heartbroken, Lydia pulled herself up despite the shock. Trying to be strong like her father, she kept moving. Opening the bedside drawer, she picked up her keys and tied her long purple hair into a bun as the sound of boots stomping through the door echoed up from the stairwell. Looking out of the window to the shady streets below, she could see military vehicles outside. She had to be quick, and so she put on some combat trousers and rushed to lace her boots.

Bang went the door, but she dared not answer.

Walking over to the closet, she fumbled with her keys – they all looked the same in this light – and with some delay she got inside and closed the door behind her.

Bang went the door again, louder this time.

"Open up," shouted an unfamiliar voice before the door smashed to pieces and soldiers entered the room, guns aimed high, ready to fire. Lydia burst through the closet door, corkscrewing through the air, and crashed into three of them like lightning. The first cracked against her shoulder as she gripped another by the throat and threw him out of the door into a crowd of other soldiers trying to pile in. She didn't have super-strength or speed, but she did have a lightweight military grade exo-suit and years of training. The suit was silver, with black wires and tubing hidden underneath the armour skeleton, accessorised with orange kneepads, shoulders and elbows.

She swung her metal fist at the third soldier, sending him flying into the wall. Leaping up, she darted through the air amidst a spray of bullets and dived behind the kitchen counter, picking up her knife block. Popping her head up, she launched every knife, ending the first two soldiers and pinning the wrist of a high-ranking soldier to the wall. He tried to reach for his pistol with his free hand, but she pinned that one too.

"Give up, your father's dead, your family's disgraced," he said trying to distract her as a grenade flew in from the corridor. She tossed it straight back, ending the rest of them in a bloom of smoke and shrapnel.

The walls caved in and flames filled the air as the alarm started roaring and sprinklers showered. The high-ranking officer who was pinned to the wall tried to get free as she walked over to him, a demonic look in her eyes. She placed a hand around his neck and lifted him high as the knife tore through his arm. She recognised the Union uniform he was wearing as he dangled in mid-air, but there was no time for questions; she crushed his neck and threw him down in rage at the fate of her father.

She packed her gear and grabbed her father's pistol and a photograph of her family from her bedside table; she could hear more footsteps approaching. Running towards the window, she smashed through and began scaling the building. The sound of sirens grew closer as she ran, jumping from roof to roof. Looking down at the city streets below, she saw officers running and cars screeching around corners. The thundering of a helicopter bellowed close by and its bright lights shone down upon her. Running fast, she jumped from roof to roof, trying to hide in the shadows, until a piece of concrete crumbled away and she lost her footing. Lydia plummeted between two buildings, an angel falling from grace. The descent felt like forever. She thought about what had happened: her mother and father. She felt the pain of his goodbyes and, in her last moment, realised she was alone, before the curb took everything away.

7

AWAKE

Far underground, in a mysterious, plain white room, an electromagnetic machine rumbled away. At its core, a pale figure hovered, outstretched in grey overalls, his arms up high, legs spread wide, head tilted in slumber. His coarse grey-blond hair had regained a golden tinge, and though he was skinny, he looked a little more solid than in days prior. Hooked up to endless tubes, his eyes fluttered as he reacted to nightmare after nightmare, vision after vision, as the machine probed his dreams, cut to his very core and performed something most inhuman.

Sam Royle was shocked back to life as his dry eyes squinted in the blinding light in front of him. An overpowering buzzing noise rumbled from below. He tried to shake his arms and legs, but they remained still. Above was a clinical white ceiling; ahead he faced a white wall, a metal chair and a thick fire door. A few bundles of cable ran along the floor and into the wall. Unable to move despite his desperate struggle, he had a headache most foul. Sam felt no weight on his feet; the strange sensation led him to believe he was levitating. As much as he wanted to move and get away, he could not, and the brightness hurt his eyes … But he felt different, so very different.

After several poor attempts to exert energy he didn't have, Sam tried to call out, but his voice was weak. No help came, and he tried to remember, think past the thick brain-fog holding him down. He remembered standing outside the therapist's office, dropping his glasses, and the man in grey telling him he would need an umbrella. Next came the mechanic, badly beaten and then taken away … and then, when he was all alone in the safety of his bedsit, the two men wearing black, who had come for him. Sam shuddered at the thought of having been kidnapped and brought to this strange place with no explanation. It scared him, angered him – and then he realised he could remember the day before, despite never normally being able to do so … and even stranger, he *wanted* to remember. Continuity of thought and memory returned to him and it brought fear and disbelief, as did the sharpness of his vision despite the lack of thick glasses in front of his eyes.

His attempts to break free were short lived, for his arms were too heavy. Movement was met with shuddering noises. His eyes adjusted to the bright light, while the humming of great machines and the ticking of a clock replaced the headache that had plagued him. Vibrations filled his mind and body; this technology felt familiar, but he did not know why.

It isn't real, he thought to himself, so accustomed to

the illusions, to the urge to return home and wish it all away.

Now that his senses were clearer, feeling flooded back. Shock and sorrow left him as he breathed as if he was taking his first breath. The mental loop plaguing his mind had gone and the fog had disappeared, replaced by an unfamiliar sense of clarity, and an obsession with the question of *why*. Left alone in a blank and empty space for hours while the clock didn't seem to change, Sam had time to contemplate, but all he had were questions – questions without answers. It was hopeless to guess who had put him here. There were no memories, no clues, no friendships, no grudges, and no sense of the past.

A few hours went by, and after a while his thoughts were interrupted by footsteps tapping down an echoing corridor in the distance; with each tap they came a little closer and he watched the door with eager anticipation. The handle came down and slowly the door opened, revealing an old man wearing a faded white lab coat, a red bowtie and a tattered grey shirt. His hair was thinning, his complexion pale, and he had dark blue eyes. The old man shuffled into the room dragging his left leg behind him. His movements were sharp yet feeble; as he closed the door and came forward, he flinched. Sam didn't greet him: he simply stared, denying that this room was anything more than an illusion. *It isn't real,* he thought, *he isn't real.*

"G-good morning," said the man. His eye twitched and he appeared to lack confidence, as if second-guessing every movement. He waved his hand in the air and the machine responded by hoisting Sam more upright. Taking a step closer, he withdrew something from his pocket with which to examine his subject.

Sam pushed and pulled with manic resistance, desperate to escape the grasp of this stranger. "Let me go! Let me go!" he shouted, but nothing he did seemed to help.

"Shh … shh. I'm not here to harm you, I-I'm here to help you," the old man stuttered, with a curious expression on his face. His attempt at reassurance seemed to be a half measure, and Sam tried to resist until he was so overcome with exhaustion; he could do nothing, now, but try to catch his breath.

"Who are you? Why am I here?" he questioned, afraid and uncertain, trying once more to break free to no avail as the machine hummed in response to his resistance.

"My name is Doctor Carter, professor of medicine, genetics, coding and neurology. You seem better already," the doctor replied with a hopeful smile which to Sam didn't seem at all appropriate. Carter used a small torch to look into each of Sam's eyes; Sam wanted to close them but watched helplessly as Carter picked up a tablet and glanced down at the screen. It was peculiar that the stranger was acting so normal, despite those characteristic flinches and twitches.

"You are safe here," he said without looking up.

"I don't feel safe, let me down, please." Hanging helplessly like this made him feel beyond dizzy.

"I'm afraid I can't, not yet: my machine is fixing you. If I turn it off now you will be brain-dead – we would reverse all the progress I have made. Think of it like a culinary dish: too soon, undercooked, too late … *burnt*."

Carter took a step back and lowered himself into the chair, where he slouched and crossed one leg over the other. He looked at Sam as if he was someone he knew, but Sam looked back in fear.

"Please, make it stop." Shaken and weak, Sam was sick of the humming; it evoked flashes of memories that were overwhelming. He wanted his meds, they would take him back, they would take it all away.

"I'm afraid it isn't that simple, and if you had any idea about the *process,* you wouldn't want me to."

"Where is the one … the one in grey? The one with the umbrella?" asked Sam with a shiver at the very thought of the last thing he could remember.

Carter looked up, unsure of what to say, as if caught by surprise. He began to write a few notes on his tablet without saying a word until muttering:

"I don't know a man in grey."

"I saw him, he warned me –"

"I don't go beyond these walls. I have no part in planning what comes in or how it comes in."

Sam was puzzled; there could be nothing more real than what he had seen, and what he had seen was the man in grey. He wondered how this peculiar stranger with his strange machine didn't know of him. Sam wondered whether his imagination was spinning another trick. He wondered whether any of it was real – he could lapse any minute and wake up back in the flat in a cold sweat. Take the pills, struggle to walk, struggle to think, in blissful ignorance. Eat, sleep and repeat.

"Are you the boss around here?"

Instead of giving an answer, Carter's eyes flicked between Sam and the tablet. He twitched once more and began to laugh before sadly shaking his head.

"What are you doing to me?"

"The mind can bend, and yours is broken. I'm putting the pieces back together, I promise you." The doctor smiled, but his smile was only as convincing as any other illusion, and Sam's mind cascaded back into every feared illusion before he realised that he could remember.

"I don't believe you; I need my pills. I ..." Sam continued to panic, and Carter calmly made his way to the corner of the room. He withdrew a bucket from a white cabinet and began to fill it with water. A few moments later, he threw the bucket over his new subject.

"Argh! What are you doing?" asked Sam, shocked and scared stiff as he shrieked and shivered.

"This – this *is* real."

"You didn't have to do that, did you? Now I'm freezing!"

"I needed you to feel, to bring yourself back, and that was the kindest thing I had on offer ..."

"Just tell me *why* I'm here, what do you want with me?"

"That is a complicated question, one without a simple answer – but there is no point lying to you." Carter withdrew Sam's notepad from his top pocket.

"You were never in an accident; you were never an addict. You were a soldier and your delusions about war were not so much delusions as truth."

Carter awaited his reaction with a kind, elderly smile that cracked with his peculiar nervous twitch. Sam looked back at him in pure disbelief. This was nonsense – how could he, this skinny wreck of a man, ever have been a soldier?

"I can barely put a key in a door, or walk, or remember. How could I ever be a soldier?"

"What they took from you, they had no right to take. But I will return it to you, I promise."

"Who? Who did this to me?"

Carter leaned forward and looked around to check that the coast was clear. "The Ministry of Men. They took your memories, intelligence and confidence. Left you in this bumbling state." Carter's words were a whisper, as if he were afraid someone would hear him. The mention of the Ministry sent a shooting pain through Sam's head, yet he could not fathom why.

"The Ministry of what?"

"They're a secret organisation that runs the world. And you carried out their bidding as a soldier."

Carter's words jogged no recollection, and Sam looked at him in confusion, as if the old man was insane.

"It doesn't really matter anymore; you're safe and I will return you to your former self." Carter's words remained to a whisper, and he looked around the room as if someone else might be listening – though Sam couldn't fathom who.

Through Sam's headache came a flurry of anger and frustration. There was a feeling he could not shake, a depression that he could not lift, but now he had some understanding.

"You are not mad. You are not some blundering burden on society – no. You have a great mind and it was taken from you."

"How many years did they take?"

"Ten, give or take."

Sam shook his head. Having had endless hallucinations, he could not believe the doctor. "No, I'm not well, and this – this isn't real." It was hard to accept, to deny everything he had ever known and put his faith in this nervous old stranger. His mind had deceived him a thousand times and he was afraid to think of himself as something more than what he was. Therapy sessions had reinforced the idea that he was damaged. The Asylum, the pain ... He was not prepared to listen to this stranger ramble on.

"You were a great man once."

Sam shook his head violently; he just wanted to leave this place, go to bed and take his pills.

"You're mistaken. There's nothing great about me, this isn't real. I'm terminally ill." Sam's disavowal was fierce; no way could he agree with anything Carter said. It was too much, it was all too much, and the humming of the machine made him feel even worse.

"My boy, if you think I'm not real, think again. You are not terminally ill; there is a fine line between mental illness and medically induced psycho-trauma. Parts of your brain were taken, and I will put them back."

"Who am I?"

"You, Samuel James Royle, are a man. You were a soldier and an engineer. But the answer, the *real* answers, would be best coming from someone who knows you."

"Well, I don't *know* anybody." As much as Sam wanted to know more, he was afraid – afraid that this stranger could be telling the truth. That maybe there was more to him than a charity case, a nobody boxed up inside day after day. Maybe he *was* something more than a skinny broken skeleton. He thought about what Carter had just said: *someone who knows you*. All he could think of was his scribbled notebook, the blotted sun, the spiralled man, the Asylum, and, most of all, the mysterious girl.

His time in the machine seemed to have given him the ability to piece certain things together: he could almost hear her voice, see her face, but it was just out of reach and the fear came straight back. She might not be real, just like the man in grey, the man at the bus stop – but still he felt one small ounce of faith. After all the therapy sessions, he had grown to accept his supposed breakdown, the supposed accident, his time in the Asylum; and yet beneath everything there remained the idea of the girl and their connection.

"I knew a girl …" he said with a small, sad, unstable smile.

"You did." Carter's reply held a hint of surprise about the successful retrieval of this memory, and Sam's heart skipped a beat.

She may be real … after all, something may be real,

thought Sam, as his heart skipped a beat. "Where is she, can you help me find her?"

"I will tell you where she is, I will tell you everything about her – but first we need something from you."

Sam didn't ask what that something was, for the idea of *her* took over everything. He would do anything to find her, see her, speak to her. He threw away all doubt about the prospect, and placed a naïve trust in Carter.

"Her name was Hope," said Carter with a smile, and the word alone unlocked a part of Sam's memory. *Hope* – he knew the name, and let it sound in his mind over and over. Carter waved his hand and Sam was lowered to the ground slowly until his toes touched the floor; the change from weightlessness to gravity felt hard, and whatever the machine had done had made him even weaker. He tried to fight his slow descent and struggled all the way to the ground. Having relied on the machine, standing was hard, but goodness knows what it was doing to him. Carter crouched over him and tried to help him up, but Sam refused.

"Let go," he said, pushing back, detesting the very thought of any assistance.

"Let me help you."

"I don't need help."

Sam tried to stagger to his feet and managed to rest on one knee, but the cold hard floor was too much and his bones felt like glass.

"Additional musculoskeletal weakness is to be

expected; it will get better with rest. I promise you, in time you will get your strength back."

"How long was I in there for?"

"Just over a day."

It did not feel like a day to Sam, it felt like forever, or an instant. He had had no perception of time until he awoke, and even then everything seemed to move incredibly slowly. Unconscious in the flat and then awake in the machine, there was no in between. Now that he was on the floor, everything was difficult. Breathing, seeing, feeling, all seemed such a chore, even more so than every day prior to today.

Carter reached into his pocket and pulled out what seemed to be a thick bar of metal; resting it upon Sam's back, he flicked a switch. Suddenly the metal expanded and began to cup his armpits. Two metal legs extended rapidly, shooting down his own legs: the thin exoskeleton thrust Sam to his feet quickly but with great care, binding to him. He took a few steps, misjudging his balance. The machine did all the work, taking all the strain as Carter moved to the door and ushered Sam to join him.

"Where are we?" asked Sam, having not thought of asking until now. He was still so dazed it was hard to comprehend anything.

"Basement level five of Infinity Research, under the East air base. Below the great Titan."

Carter's answer sent a spark through Sam's brain; he remembered something of this from his past. The name was familiar – he had known this place as a boy. Despite having no memory of his late teenage years or the *acci-*

dent, he remembered distant things about his childhood. Infinity Research, however, was not somewhere he would ever want to visit, not even in memory, and so he began to panic, hyperventilate and go very pale.

"My parents worked here; they were prisoners here. My therapist said this place didn't exist, that there was no record of it existing. I shouldn't be here, I have to leave, I –" Sam tried to catch his breath, his vision blurred, and the impending doom of another blip took hold until Carter placed a hand upon his shoulder.

"That's it, that's it. Look at me," Carter said with an avuncular smile. Sam controlled his breath and, for the first time ever, didn't blip after all. He took a moment to come back, to take everything in as Carter continued. "I'm sorry I didn't say anything sooner, but I thought it was better to wait. Jonathan and Elizabeth did work here, and I knew them well." There was sadness in Carter's tone as he held the door. It hurt him to speak of those he had loved and lost.

Sometimes Sam felt them standing nearby or looking down on him. Sometimes he missed them, sometimes he cursed them, but in truth he'd never known them; they had made the decision to leave him forever, and for that, how could he forgive them? Sadly, they were more an idea than anything else, an idea lost through war and experimentation. Sam tried to think about them for a moment, about this place, about Hope, about everything, but all he could find was darkness.

"I didn't think you would remember this place, and

that is progress. In all honesty it's a miracle – can you walk?"

"I only remember the name … and I can try."

Carter gave a nod and led Sam down a bleak white corridor. Quiet and lonely, there was no one else around, as if this place was his and his alone; but the further Sam walked the more he felt like he was being watched. He thought of his parents, the little he knew of them and how they'd dedicated their lives to this place. He thought of Hope, and how the idea of her was everything. Despite it all seeming like a dream, he had nothing to believe but his feelings, so he pushed on with Carter, this old peculiar stranger who had given him the gift of memory. Although he was afraid, Sam swallowed his fear. He had to get better, had to discover who he once was.

8

BROTHERS AND SISTERS

It was the middle of the night; Nathan's convoy flew down the open road towards the city and many things were on his mind. He had let Jacobs get too close and he promised himself it would never happen again. As the truck rumbled on, every couple of minutes the static of the radio brought a different voice. "Confirmed," they said, and each one was a tick on Nathan's overdue checklist. The Union had done what had been promised, yet he could not help but obsess over the burden placed upon him. His enemies had been dealt with, but some were friends; he knew their families, he had dined with them, laughed with them – and now they were gone.

Covering distance through the night, they passed various outposts and raids. Closer to the city, lawlessness was rampant, whole blocks up in flames. The public rallied at district gates and such anarchy provided the perfect cover for Nathan to deal with his enemies. Control officers who had been overwhelmed on the streets were now backed by Union soldiers who met the public with gunshots and tear gas, forcing them back into hiding. Then Nathan instructed his newly acquired Union soldiers to detain thousands of activists and troublemakers. They went building to building, door to door, dragging out suspected terrorists long held on watch lists. Resistance met a swift and violent end.

Caleb remained quiet as they passed legions of soldiers; he accepted what tonight was, a massacre of ideology. Nothing else mattered anymore, he was alone except for the familiar orders, and that was how his life had been for too long. He had never been one to ask about the Ministry or the Great Houses, they were just more names and places. Caleb wasn't from Sovereign; he was raised in the Kingdom's Western Quadrant, a quiet and peaceful farming state, now dry. He didn't care about the state of Sovereign, but he did care about traffic and multiple roadblocks, which popped up every hundred metres. The endless spotlights, signalling and whistles. The specks of blood on the windscreen that the wipers seemed to miss – that infuriated him the most as he tried to concentrate on the road.

They moved forward until they reached Nathan's apartment. Armed guards were stationed outside the property and at the ends of the street. Neither of them had said a word to each other; Caleb knew about Evelyn and the Union's threat, and saw how it was affecting Nathan, but he himself was too rough and bitter to give any advice.

It was time for Nathan to depart. As he opened the

truck door ready to step down, Caleb grabbed him by the shoulder.

"Whatever you do, Nathan, don't dwell on it."

"I won't," Nathan replied before climbing down from the truck. He had to take a second look at the two Union soldiers outside, their grey uniforms and Crane insignia on their armour. He remembered fighting a man in such armour and killing him with his bare hands, but he tried to repress the memory as he made for his door. The truck rolled away as he took off his gloves, jacket and even his boots. For a moment he remained on the porch, afraid to go inside, afraid to face what he had done.

Everything became so real as he put his key in the door and then headed up the stairs ever so quietly, hoping Rose would be fast asleep. In his marble bathroom he removed the armoured vest. The weight lifted from his shoulders and he could breathe again.

Nathan undressed, revealing his heavy build, the shrapnel scars on his chest and the one that ran down his back. Stun burns were scattered on his shoulders and his wrists. In the mirror he stared for a long time at the man he had become. The adrenaline was wearing off, but he wasn't tired. He washed his face to cool down, but in the reflection, in the corner of his eye, all he could see was the insignia of the Crane and he tried his best to block Evelyn from his mind. Numb but wide awake, he wanted nothing more than to join Rose as she rested, but right now it was impossible. Not yet, not with everything going on, and everything on his mind.

He locked himself in his soundproof study, where

most of his time had been spent over the past few days, the most secure room in the house. Nathan hadn't really eaten, and there was no time to think. If he stopped now, he would have to look back at the damage he had done. Though his part in it all was minimal, he couldn't help worrying about the Council. They were reckless; destroying the Great Houses without warning had forced this situation upon him, and he felt a fool for not foreseeing what he was getting into. The need for something quick and sharp to help him calm down took over, and he drew his hip flask to take a sweet warming burn. It tasted just like the old days – but time had passed, and he turned to the windowsill to see how fast it went. There he found the red rose, brown and dry.

The earpiece upon his desk gave off a dull blue light: a call was coming through. Nathan stared down at the desk and wondered to what extent Chief Councillor Rogan's spies were monitoring him; but he pushed his concerns aside, sat down and took the call.

"Nathan, I assume the military operations have gone as expected."

"Yes, my Council. Our opposition has been disposed of," he said with some reservation.

"Excellent, the Council gives its blessing; we await your arrival – but there is something of concern."

"What is it, my Council?"

"Evelyn Owen … I'm sorry it had to go the way it did but there was no alternative. I hope you understand it was for the greater good."

The name brought Nathan to a standstill and he chose his words wisely, playing the game. "It is no concern of mine," he said, all the while looking at the tainted rose on his windowsill.

"There is no room for remorse in our new world. Now, you know what I'm going to ask you – the Titan: for twenty years it has lain dormant, we need it operational."

"It will be."

"Well, the clock is ticking; rest and I will speak to you early tomorrow."

Nathan had bluffed under pressure: having never seen it for himself he knew the formula was far from perfect, and he needed time, time he didn't have. Rogan terminated the transmission and Nathan was left wondering about his next move. He felt desperate; the Titan hadn't been airborne in twenty years … but he had a plan. A second transmission came through in his earpiece to interrupt his train of thought.

"Sir?" said a rather nervous officer on the other end.

"What is it?"

"The list is done, every name."

"Good."

"There was one problem ..."

"We don't have time for problems."

"Someone who wasn't technically on *the* list … Jacob's daughter, sir, she's Special Forces, she's, she's –"

"Alive." Nathan sighed. He didn't have the energy for anger, impatience or even worry. He lacked the ability to care – what was one small mistake after everything that had happened? Still, Rogan's words echoed in his mind; no stone unturned.

"She escaped; she wore her father's suit. Ten men died trying to –"

"We have an ex-Special Forces fighter with a motive and high-tech gear. Find her, kill her."

"Yes, sir."

Nathan dropped the Union handset down on his desk and checked the time. It was four in the morning, time to get out of the chair and into bed, try to rest. The liquor had helped a little, but as he walked over to his bed his stomach was still sore from the impact of Jacob's stray bullets. Rose lay facing away from him, a sleeping angel, and he climbed into bed trying not to make a noise. He turned to his bedside table and took a pill to help him sleep, gulping it down with a glass of water. He laid his head down and soon he was out. His rest, however, didn't last long, as about two hours later Rose shuffled around restlessly and woke him.

"I had a bad dream, Nathan," she said.

Nathan moved closer and placed his arm around her. "What happened?" he asked, brushing his hand over her cheek.

"They tried to take you away from me, they took everything away from me."

"Nothing's going to happen to you, Rose, or to us. I promise."

His mind was certain as he held her close. No one would ever take anything from him, not today, not ever.

～

Nathan hated sleep, and the pills helped only so much. He was a light sleeper and only needed a few hours; when he did go to sleep it was always just a short time before the memories of war and bad deeds disturbed him. This particular morning, however, was very different to most, and thought he slept through until the morning, he would never be ready for what awaited him.

Rose woke up first and flicked on the TV. To her disbelief, pictures of the Great Houses and the faces of the dead were all over the news. She dragged herself forward to grip the metal frame at the end of the bed, and to her dismay she saw Evelyn. Her best friend, her maid of honour and soon-to-be godmother of her child, was no more. Tears rolled down Rose's cheeks as she became crushed by disbelief and despair. She didn't want to believe any of it.

There was nothing worse for Nathan than the heart-break of hearing her reaction; then came the report and the names being listed. He remained still, unsure of what to do, as they echoed through his mind one after the other and he remained hidden in the duvet away from the world he had awoken to. Rose couldn't speak, could barely breathe; the shock had broken her heart.

"Evelyn's dead, Nathan – they're all dead!" she shouted, and Nathan stayed hidden as the sound of her cries made it all too real. He turned over to see her in such pain, writhing in disbelief, unable to accept the news.

"I know," he replied, trying to place his arm around her to protect her, to tell her that everything would be okay. "I found out late last night; the country fell into chaos; I couldn't wake you."

Rose tried to dry her tears, but they kept flooding. "We were like sisters – *sisters*, and she's gone! Just like that, she's gone …"

She began to panic and struggled to breathe; it was all too much. Nathan took both her arms and looked into her eyes. "Look at me, Rose, try to breathe, you have to be strong."

She trembled, looking very pale, unable to speak. Her heart was breaking as tears thundered down. Her first thought wasn't to blame him, and Nathan was more sorry than she would ever know. He placed a gentle arm around her to hide his guilt and wished it all away, the threat of the Union, the fear of the fire – but it wasn't going anywhere. He had a plan in his mind, well thought out, meticulous; all he had to do was stick to it and they might just get through this.

"The terrorists responsible have been arrested, they will pay for what they've done, Rose." The words left his lips, but it didn't feel like he had said them.

"What sort of evil could do this? What sort of evil would kill them? Revenge will never bring her back; Evelyn would never have wanted it."

Rose was right – in her kind, sweet way she was right, and she would never think that Nathan had had a hand in any of it. Her words, her trust, her bloodshot eyes shamed him. He felt the full weight of his mistakes; ever since he'd agreed to the Union's bargain, things had escalated so far out of control that the lies and secrets were burying him.

"The worst of men," he said, unable to look her in the eye; then he sat up sharply to seize his opportunity. "We aren't safe here, Rose, we must leave the Kingdom."

"Leave? Nathan, you're scaring me."

"It isn't safe her anymore, it isn't safe for you or me or the baby. I have connections in the Union who can save us, but we must leave immediately." Nathan pushed back her hair and lifted her chin. He looked into her angelic eyes, put on a brave face and stroked her swollen belly with his hand. He was half lying, but it was a half-truth, too, smothered by guilt-ridden sadness.

"How can you think of leaving? We need to stay close to the hospital," she replied, pushing his hand away as the tears continued to rain.

"The Union has the best medical facilities; you know it's the safest place for us. We need to go soon – it's a matter of days." It was time to leave and become a part of something bigger, for reasons he couldn't admit to. The Union Council loomed above his shoulders, his bad deeds weighing him down.

"No, we can't. I won't; not before the funeral at least." Though her voice trembled, her mind was made up. Rose was stubborn, and distraught from the loss of a loved one. Nathan had not thought of the funeral at all.

"We are in danger; the riots are spreading and I can't hold on much longer. I don't know who to trust. I'm afraid, Rose."

"Is that the answer to all of this: fear? To run away? Evelyn would have hated that. Evelyn would have been brave, stood her ground." She was right, Evelyn would have stayed to save her people, to make a difference, no matter how small.

"You and the baby are the most important things to me, and I have to do everything necessary to keep us safe."

"I'm not leaving. Not now, not after this. We need to stay for the funeral, for Evelyn and for our child. He will be born in Sovereign." Rose stroked her bump and tried to be brave. "I know you worry about us, but this is our home … and I'm worried about you."

"You're worried about me?" he said in surprise whilst trying to wipe a tear from her eye.

"I know your job isn't pretty. I know there are things going on that you can't talk about, but I see pain in you. No matter how much you try to hide it, I can see it. You haven't been yourself for weeks, you haven't even mentioned Drake, your best friend. You won't talk about anything – I need you to talk," Rose sobbed, but tried to stay strong, strong for Evelyn, strong for the child.

Nathan hated to see her so upset, hated to see her worry; it was the only thing that could break his outer shell.

"I know, I know," he gulped in agreement, afraid to face his true friend. What was done seemed a dream, far from reality. He wondered whether stopping it was possible, whether there was another way. Right now, there seemed no other option. He had to see Drake no matter how hard it might be, but right now even that seemed just another part of his operation. Although the publicised reports made Nathan out to be a hero, Drake was smart, and understood the level of propaganda he was faced with.

"I will see him, I promise," Nathan said, ready to face anything for her.

"I want to go with you."

"No, it's too dangerous. You need to stay here under protection."

He could not let her do that, no matter how much she wanted to. They embraced; she buried her head in his chest and he rested his chin on her shoulder.

Before long it was time for him to go. Nathan got ready and before leaving he went past his office to get his coat. There he stopped and looked at the photograph on his desk. The four of them, so young, so full of hope and promise. When he stared into a mirror and saw a different man.

There was a knock on the door; his convoy was waiting. He made his way outside, nodded at the guards, and got in.

The drive to the Owen residence took forever, past endless checkpoints and Union uniforms. Nathan trembled, and for the first time in his life he didn't know what to say. *He doesn't know,* he said to himself over and over.

Earlier that day in the Owen household, Drake had been in a dark place. He had waited all evening for her return as thoughts drifted through his head: *Maybe she's stuck in the office; maybe she's in traffic.* All he could think about was their last conversation when he turned on the news and saw her face amongst those confirmed dead. Crumbling to his knees, he smashed his fists on the floor, kicked in the kitchen counters and tore out cupboards, desperate to take it all away. The explosion had shattered everything that he held dear, and no matter how hard he kicked or how loud he screamed, her death remained real.

Drake sat drinking heavily on the floor all night and through the morning. His eyes were bloodshot and his lips stained with cigarettes. He glanced at photo albums and listened to voicemails on repeat, picturing her ghost. Guards were positioned outside, but he hadn't even noticed as he lost himself like any caring man would in a situation beyond awful.

When Nathan arrived in his limousine, he found a very different man inside the Owens' Cotswold stone townhouse. A very different man to the one in the photograph of the four of them from ten years earlier. Nathan left his gun on the seat and stepped out of the car as the driver held the door.

"Do you require any assistance, sir?" said the Union guard before opening his jacket slightly to reveal a pistol.

"No thank you, I will be quite alright."

Nathan approached the door, but no one answered. With a push it opened, and he walked in. He stared into the dark hallway and closed the door behind him. Peering into the front room – what a state it was. Cigarette packets, bottles, and photo albums covered the floor. The stench was of smoke and stale alcohol. He moved on through to the kitchen and found that was the same: cupboard doors ripped off, mess everywhere. Every bit of this Nathan felt he had caused; he could only imagine what was going through Drake's mind, what he may have driven him to.

"Drake, Drake," he called out, but received no response and so feared the worst. When Nathan was most off guard, Drake came fast from behind the door, heavy breathing and foul breath accompanying his manic red-eyed stagger.

"You killed her, you fucking killed her!" Drake shouted, pushing Nathan away; then he withdrew a kitchen knife from his dressing gown.

"Drake, it wasn't me!"

"Liar! Stay away from me!"

Nathan stared at the kitchen knife glistening in his friend's hand, watching it tremble, sharp and dangerous. As easy as taking it and putting him down would be, he remained calm and still.

"I found those responsible, I took care of them," Nathan lied.

"You would say anything – *anything*," replied Drake, bitter and twisted, driven mad with loss.

"Just give me the knife – I promise you, I tried to help."

Drake shook his head; there was a subtle change in his expression when he heard those words, but he charged at him nevertheless. Stepping to the side, Nathan caught his sleeve with one hand and opened Drake's hand with the other, before easing him to the floor. Nathan placed the knife in his pocket as Drake held his head in his hands and the tears came. He stayed quiet for a while, before getting up and staggering out of the room and back into the living room, where he retrieved a half-full bottle of wine and took a large swig before falling onto the couch. Nathan followed close behind, anxious about the pain he had caused and what might come next.

"I know what it looks like, I'm so sorry," he said – and he was; he wished it could be different.

Drake had seen the broadcasts, the fire, the arrests, the pictures of her as the nation mourned, and still he felt there was more to it than met the eye. He was unable to look at Nathan and just stared down at the coffee table, keeping his eyes averted from the mess around him.

"You could have stopped this, why didn't you stop this?"

"I-I couldn't. I was betrayed. They came for me, too; they came for Rose."

It hurt to lie again today, and Nathan sank down on the arm of the sofa, careful not to get too close – he had never seen Drake quite like this. There had been a few times before when Nathan had taken him to rehab, but nothing like this. Before, he was just hurting himself; now something real had taken everything, something he couldn't change, and that crushed him.

"I just don't understand – you tried to tell me she was in danger; I should have listened to you. Tell me what happened. Tell me and promise me you will tell the truth."

The truth, Nathan thought. Everything flashed

through his mind: battlefields, Baylor, his election, the government's talk of a tribunal, the Ministry of Men, desperation, Cat, Rogan and the Union Crane. It had all been sparked by the Great Houses burning to the ground. He pushed away every truth and thought hard about what the *truth* had become. He had rehearsed the answer in his head dozens of times on the way here, but that did not make it any easier to get the words out. Here was his only true friend, one of the only two people he could ever trust, and it hurt.

"My generals burnt down the Great Houses and the Old Abbey, then they tried to come for me but failed." It was hard to say, it pained Nathan. Even though Drake stared with dark, damaged eyes, almost impossible to lie to, Nathan had lied all the same.

"Why didn't you stop them?" asked Drake, trembling. "Why didn't you stop them?" he pleaded, a broken man.

"There's nothing I could have done; I didn't know until it was too late. The Union Council saved me, and I promise you that those responsible will suffer until the end."

Nathan had expected talk of revenge to make Drake feel better, give him a sense of peace, but he was unmoved.

"I just wish it had been me," Drake confessed as tears ran down his cheeks. Nathan realised he had never seen him cry until today. "I just wish I could trade her life for mine, for I'm weak, and I deserve it and she didn't." The thought of revenge didn't enter Drake's mind; all he wanted to do was turn back time and be a better man for her. If he could have changed their last conversation, made it all better, maybe he would not feel such guilt hanging over his head.

"Don't be so hard on yourself, please."

"I'm trying, but I can't help it. She's gone, she's really gone –"

"Please let me know if there's anything I can do for you, anything I can do to help."

Drake took a minute to ponder; he smiled in remembrance of her, bringing his sobbing to an end. He looked into Nathan's eyes, really looked into them, and thought about what his wife had said about his oldest friend. With sudden fury and suspicion, he got to his feet and threw the coffee table at the wall. The glass shattered and photographs scattered on the floor. Nathan made a small hand signal at the window behind Drake's back to tell his men that everything was under control and that he was not in harm's way.

"The *brave* Nathan Sahl," Drake sniffled, staggering towards him, "worshipped for bringing terrorists to justice whilst betraying those who loved him. How can you sleep at night? How did you not know they were going to do this?"

"I didn't know, I didn't know, and I'm sorry, I-I should've seen it coming."

"I don't believe you. There's nothing you can say to fix this, nothing in the world you could ever do. You will bear her death for the rest of your days. I don't want you to be here." Drake could not look at him as Nathan moved towards him and hesitated, unsure of what to do.

"Get yourself some rest, please. The funeral is tomorrow. Be strong, Drake, you have to trust me." Nathan placed a pistol on the table, a few hundred Sovereigns and a fresh pack of cigarettes, as Drake gave him a disgusted and unforgiving stare. "And be careful," Nathan continued as he backed away slowly, leaving the pistol as a show of trust.

"Get out," Drake replied.

"Rose wants to see you tomorrow; you have to be strong."

"Get out," Drake said once more, looking more menacing than ever.

Nathan backed out of the room feeling the full weight of his decision; he couldn't tell the truth or say how he really felt. He was angry – angry at the Union Council – but it was a venomous and quiet anger. They had only done what they always did, made someone else do their dirty work, and unfortunately, this time, it was him. He would be in their pocket, under watchful eyes, for the rest of his days; one wrong step and it would all be over.

Nathan had betrayed his past, his friendship, and, out of desperation, lied to someone he had never lied to before, for they had been brothers. He made for the door and headed out into a bright new day while Drake remained in darkness.

Drake waited before going to the window and lifting the blind to watch him go. The brightness of day strained his eyes. He had not seen daylight for a while, and it was beautiful, but not for him, as a dark cloud had gathered above the Owen household.

The Union military convoy awaited Nathan's return. Nathan headed down the steps, followed by watchful eyes. Drake only saw one set of eyes as Nathan walked to the limousine, and they were those of Caleb Walker, a dangerous man of few words. His eyes were war-torn, black and cold as they stared back at Drake without empathy. Drake was too afraid to watch them any longer, so he retreated from the window to stew and simmer, and to continue his descent into darkness.

9

TORN APART

When Nathan closed the door, Drake was alone again. Locked in a spiral of decay, he lay for hours staring at the blank ceiling, contemplating everything. He did not dare venture upstairs to their bedroom or the bathroom, there were too many things to remind him of the sweet soul he had lost. His heart was heavy and numb, having cried, cursed and screamed – nothing was going to bring her back. Alone now, as if for the first time, the shallow words of his best friend did nothing to make him feel better. Drake would be a fool to think Nathan wasn't hiding something, he was always hiding something, but it was impossible to imagine him doing anything to cause Evelyn harm. Drake still felt that his best friend cared for those close to him and would do anything to protect them, despite his faults.

There was no peace for Drake now, he felt unable to move until it was dark, and by then he was starving, and all out of drink. The pills wore off and he needed something stronger, much stronger. Something that could make him forget.

He put on a navy mac over his rather worn grey suit and stared out of the window; part of him didn't want to go outside but his body gave him little choice. He plucked up the courage to open the door and walked down the steps, where two very young and inexperienced cadets were attempting to stand guard.

"Where are you going, sir?" asked the tall skinny one with a rather frightened gulp.

"I'm going for a walk," replied Drake. He went to step past them, but the short round cadet stepped into his path.

"We have orders to make sure you don't go anywhere, sir."

The cadet adjusted his collar with a sheepish look before clearing his throat. Drake stepped closer. "I see … Do you know who visited my house earlier today?" The cadets nodded in unison but didn't say anything. "Well?"

"The C-Chief, sir."

"C-correct, the Chief. Now, I'm leaving, and if you try to stop me or try to follow me, I will see to it that your Chief has you scrubbing bodies for the rest of your days."

"Our orders are to watch your house, sir, and that's what we'll do." The young cadets turned toward the brickwork and didn't move an inch.

Drake walked south through security gate after

security gate, leaving the cadets to bicker amongst themselves. Other soldiers didn't stop him either, for his community pass allowed the most unrestricted form of travel. Nathan had restored order to Sovereign in such a ruthless fashion. An iron fist had quashed the riots almost overnight and any faction that had dared to roam the streets now remained indoors.

The cold, fresh air did Drake good for a short time, and on the surface it seemed as though he was making progress. His mind, however, was damaged. It felt like someone was watching him, but there was not a soul around; maybe it was just the evening chill of the wind rustling the trees and shaking the lampposts. For miles he walked down quiet streets; the odd community control officer and soldier passed him, but when they stopped him, his name did more than keep them at bay. One or two laughed and joked about how he was heading in the wrong direction, that the road he was on wasn't safe, but he did not care – there was only one thing on his mind, and nothing would get in his way.

Wandering for miles without a care for his own safety, the further he walked the more the neighbour-hood changed around him, from a safe part of the city to the first high-rise towers. Drake found himself on the border of the Commons. The wind carried the smell of fire, sewage and sickness; he smelt the smoke and heard the song of sirens. It knocked him sick. It had been years since he had crossed the line and felt safe; someone of his status risked everything heading into the Commons.

Grey high-rise after high-rise, poorly constructed, ill maintained and overpopulated, spoilt the view. The line demarcating this district was the definition of a divide, a contrast as visible as night and day. At the crossroads were the remains of makeshift walls, now broken down and covered in graffiti. It was a foolish move for someone of his stature to go beyond the walls. Fifty years ago, when the authorities tried to crack down on drugs and crime, the residents built walls all around the Commons, barricading themselves in. The fight went on for ten days as hooligans threw petrol bombs from the walls above. The government gave up: the intervention wasn't worth the cost. If it had happened now, Nathan would have broken down the walls in minutes; thirty years ago was a different time.

"Mister Owen, Mister Owen!" Drake heard a shout from behind him; it was the two cadets, waving and running towards him. Drake ignored their cries; he crossed the road and pushed himself through a gap in the fence. He stumbled and tore his jacket on a sharp piece of metal, almost falling into a ditch. When he made his way out of the bushes and regained his balance, he was on a street with burnt-out cars, smashed windows and people sleeping around barrel fires. It was another world where the sound of loud music blaring and people howling never stopped. Crowds of youths scoured the neighbourhood. He would never have come here before, and if he had, he would have kept his head down in case of being mugged, but now he was not afraid. Everything had been taken from him and there was nothing left to fear.

Drake kept walking a lonely road, turned a few corners and found himself surrounded by nightlife. There were small huddles of people. Some staring, sizing him up, and others going about their business. One of the men stood alone with his hood up, leaning against a wall covered in bad graffiti. Shaking and coughing, he seemed like a dealer. Drake strode over to him, his shoulders hunched and hiding his face in his collar. The dealer smiled with lit-up eyes in the flickering street-light. Drake looked at the dealer's hands: his fingertips looking almost bruised – just the sign he was after.

"You look lost, far from home," said the dealer. Others stared now and began to approach before the man gave them a signal to back away.

"I need some glass; can you hook me up?" Drake asked, trying his best to seem street without stretching the act too far. The thug looked him up and down, unsure of what to make of such a high-status customer.

"Trust me, you don't want what I got; shit will change you. Go home to your mansion and have another chicken dinner. You have a mansion and a chicken dinner or two, don't you?"

"I don't have – anything to go home to," replied Drake. It was clear by the look in his eyes that he was troubled, so the dealer took pity on him.

"Three hundred it'll cost."

"What?" Drake asked in shock, afraid of being ripped off, "I just saw someone buy for fifty."

"Prices are relative, my man; fifty for the poor, three hundred for the rich – redistribution of wealth, you understand?"

It took Drake some time to reason with himself. For a moment there was the same resistance in his mind that he'd wrestled with daily before today, but now the want took over.

"Okay," he replied. Pulling out his wallet, he handed over some of the cash Nathan had given him, and the man returned something heavy, wrapped in a piece of foil. Steam rolled off it before Drake put it in his pocket.

"Don't you get that shit out now, ya hear me? Now get out of here."

Drake nodded and began to walk away. It had been five years – five whole years without it. He walked a bit further and then turned down an alleyway, crooked and narrow. He pulled out the foil and a light mist emerged from within. It was a crisp purple glass rock, cool crystal, bright as could be, heavy and hard; but if you stared too long it would disappear. Palms sweating, the anticipation of euphoria followed, the wish for sweet release. Drake stared, forgetting every previous down and idolising every past high.

He pulled off a speck with a bare hand; it always burnt the skin and made it easy to spot a fellow user. After stuffing the rest away, he pressed it to his nose and began to sniff. As the ball hit his hand it became like liquid nitrogen except it wasn't cold: it floated, evaporated, steamed and soared into his nostrils, within an instant creating a buzz unlike any other. His pupils dilated, his heart pounded, as every worry melted away. The need to smoke, dance, smile and live filled his brain to the brim, but he remained cool – a veteran, after all. It was as if nothing bad had ever happened ...

Five years ... but Drake knew his route: he was a stone's throw from the dirtiest bar this side of town and he was walking fast, storming down the road with an energy he had missed. On Seventh was Hollow, bright purple lights in a street alive and lawless. Prostitutes, drug dealers, gang members. Community control and the military wouldn't come down here; it was run by the remnants of underground gangs. Some said the Commons ran by night and dried up during the day.

Hollow was the dirtiest bar this side of town, where you were free to be whoever you wanted. You could dance, sell, smoke, sniff, gamble. Even rent a room for a small price, though the sheets were never clean. The music was blaring as Drake walked inside and kept his head down. Security didn't stop him; it would be foolish to turn down anyone with Drake's money to burn. Wading into darkness, through doorways and thick curtains, Drake meandered into the underworld. It was a crowded building, with caverns and passageways, and he made his way straight to the main dance floor. By now the glass was in full flow and faces began to blur past him; it was as if he was floating without feeling. Through the crowd, Drake approached the bar and stared past the barman at glass bottles that began to shake. Feeling loose, he forgot who he was, his heart-breaks and torments. He ordered shot after shot, but after the glass alcohol did little. A burning feeling claimed his chest; he was floating. Nothing could wipe the smile off his face as he fell in love with the music and the people around him despite being so out of place.

Bright strobe lights burned into his brain. Hypnotic, they spoke a foreign language to him as he sat and watched, taking in every feeling. Time drifted away as he was lost in the colours of the violent pink and green strobe lights. He felt at one with the world, but as quickly as it began it started to wear off. After wonder came the fear. He caught a glimpse of Evelyn's ghost in the crowd, and then it went away, lost in a blur. Drake blinked, wiped his eyes, looked again as he saw her smile, then saw it was another girl. His heart sank and his pulse quickened as the glass's first phase wore off. Having only done a little, he needed more, much more, and he began to panic before reminding himself that the feeling would soon be back. The place felt too warm and sweat melted from his brow as a skeletal hand came down upon his shoulder.

"Drake." The familiar voice brought him back to reality, a voice he recognised but in his sorry state he could not put a name to. He turned around in slow-motion to see a blurred figure; it took him time to focus, but when he could he knew who it was.

"Arnold, what are you doing here?" slurred Drake. The old driver looked rough, having lost his tie and suit jacket; his white shirt was stained and dirty. Petrified, he kept turning to look over his shoulder.

"Drake! You have to help me; they are looking for me," he pleaded, gripping him by the collar. Drake looked at him, unsure of whether this was real; it was hard to hear amidst the music and he was not in the right state of mind for the situation.

"Who is looking for you?"

"Last night, my missus told me not to come home, said they were looking for me, so I slept in the limousine. I came here because *they* can't come in here."

"Who was looking for you?" Drake asked again; it was hard to make sense of anything right now, but he knew something was wrong, that Arnold was in trouble. Arnold's pleas for help sobered Drake severely and he stared into the eyes of his driver eagerly anticipating an answer; but he seemed almost too afraid to speak.

"They made me give it to her, said they would kill me if I didn't, said it was just a letter, but it, it …" Arnold was distraught, overcome with guilt. It wasn't like him to be sad or afraid, he was a sweet old man at heart, but right now he was haunted. Drake clenched his fists and gritted his teeth, but he couldn't feel anything, and the room was still spinning.

"Who?" he asked, but in the back of his mind he already knew.

"A woman, an invisible woman."

Drake felt like he was dreaming. It was preposterous, beyond ridiculous, and for a moment his heart sank, overcome with guilt at the thought that his friend may have been to blame. "You aren't making any sense, Arnold," he said as he brushed the glass to reassure himself.

"There's something else. I'm being followed … but I recognise him."

"It's all just your imagination, isn't it? I don't need this."

"Walker. Caleb Walker."

The name caught in the back of Drake's throat, cold as ice. It hit him hard and without mercy – in that moment he knew that Nathan was involved. Arnold had confirmed everything Drake had feared Nathan capable of; their entire friendship, their history meant nothing.

"How could Nathan do this? How could he?" Drake made no effort to contain himself; he had gone pale and a part of him had died.

"I'm sorry, please forgive me," begged Arnold.

"Forgive you? She trusted you. You took away the *only* thing I ever loved! Evelyn was good, she was kind, she was too good for this world, how could you do this to us?"

"He said he would kill my wife, my son. You would do the same thing in my position."

"Get the fuck out of here," said Drake as he signalled to the bartender for another.

"Please, you don't understand. I was as good as dead either way."

It was too late; Drake turned his back and Arnold walked away. Drake swayed on the stool as the glass entered its second phase. As soon as Arnold went, Drake forgot all about the encounter; he leant back on the bar stool as his mind disappeared and hovered above him. Hours passed by, people came and went but he remained like a statue. Swaying, then, in a hypnotic state, he began to drool on the bar. It wasn't long before security had him, but unlike most, they did not steal his things.

Drake didn't know what was going on until he fell through the floor into an abyss stretching forever. The blackness was good until his head was pounding against the wet sticky floor. A deep sadness and heavy heart brought him back as the bouncers gripped his arms tight and pulled him up. Thrown out into the rain, he stumbled; it seemed impossible to stand, for glass tended to take away your legs on the come-down. He managed to stumble down some of the most dangerous streets in Sovereign, probably mistaken for some drug lord, given the way he was dressed. It was in an alleyway just south of Hollow where the sobering pains took hold. Everything seemed so surreal as he cackled to himself before bending down to spew a putrid purple vomit; and then he saw something horrifying. A pair of feet stuck out from a large pile of garbage bags.

His hair stood on end; the black shoes didn't move. When he got closer, he recognised the black trousers and white shirt. It was nArold, cold and lifeless in a pool of blood, his face fixed cold and pale in fear. Drake froze; his heart beat out of his chest and he took off fast. All the way through the Commons he did not stop, all the way to the fence line and beyond. He could feel watchful eyes behind him the entire time, but he didn't turn around. Straight home he ran whilst dark thoughts raced through his mind. Out of breath, he locked the doors, checked every room, and sat downstairs, unable to go back into the bedroom for the memory of her. Staring down at the gun on the table, he hesitated before picking it up. It was so heavy. All he could think about was betrayal, revenge and suicide. Then he got the urge, the uncontrollable itch. Scouring his jacket for the remaining glass, he ripped it from the foil, held it to his nose and sniffed. His eyes went black as he fell back onto the couch in a deep, dark sleep.

10

THE LABORATORY

At Infinity Research, on the fifth floor below ground, Sam staggered to control the metal supports assisting his walking. Getting used to the suit wasn't easy: the balance, movement and weightlessness were odd. The white corridor was long and there was no pace in Doctor Carter. He was old, slow and hunched, and walking as if in a dream, flinching unexpectedly every now and then. Many reinforced doors lined the corridor; each one opened and closed as they passed. No noise above or below – they were completely alone but for their own footsteps. An eerie feeling filled the place and Sam didn't like it one bit. *Where are the guards? Where are the soldiers?* he thought as he passed the endless doors.

"Where is everyone?" he finally plucked up the courage to ask. He wondered who was watching the cameras that moved with them, and how many other floors there were.

"We are five storeys below ground, safe from the world above."

"How long have you been down here?"

"Too long."

Carter's answers seemed vague; something about him did not add up, but he looked at Sam with an honest face. Doubting the man who had brought him back was hard.

"I have been here for a very long time and will be until my work is finished. There's too much to do and not enough time."

"What work?"

Carter hunched some more and took to a whisper. "Oh, big science things and all that lark. Much has happened since you fell asleep. Union guards walk the corridors. They speak of riots and murders; there is something brewing on the surface, though I can't be sure what it is."

Carter feared the worst, he was running out of time and the surveillance meant it was hard for him to say what he wanted to. But Sam lacked the ability to care about anything right now; the surface was the least of his worries. It was hard to concentrate on anything at all for the plain white walls around him. Ahead was a large, reinforced door that opened to reveal a corridor where two heavily armoured guards stood in an unsettling silence. Carter hobbled past without acknowledging their presence, but Sam stared and, though he could not see eyes through their visors, he felt them staring back at him. Something wasn't right, something made him feel on edge. The sight of the heavy doors, cameras and guns made him uneasy. Whatever Carter was, he was not free.

Another corridor, another glass door halfway down. On closer inspection it was thick and strong, and upon passing through Sam realised that they could be for keeping something or someone *in*. The corridor continued past the door until finally opening out into a vast room full of strange wonders that could distract anyone with half an interest in science.

The chamber was filled with great machines, boxes and computer parts. There were high shelves all around the room filled with maps and designs, chemicals. It was a scientist's playground, a laboratory. Amongst all its wonders, something stood out to Sam above all else. Some sort of robot, about five feet tall, though hunched and dormant now; Sam placed his hand on its armour, which felt light as a feather. Black and grey with hints of white, it had a face but no signs of life in its eyes.

"I feel like I've seen one before, a long time ago … I always thought they were taller," said Sam, staring into the dark red sensory units, once bright with colour.

"Its name was D39, he was never quite ready for combat. The others were taller, much taller. Large enough for a soldier to control from the inside, but not this one, this one was different, do you know why?"

"No …"

"This was your mother and father's work before the war was over," said Carter with pride.

"My mother and father were traitors."

Sam didn't think of them often; they were among the few memories that had survived his illness; he was six when he last saw them. Carter walked up to the Mech and placed his palm in its hand, his head hung in sadness.

"I am proud to say I did know Jonathan and Elizabeth and they were not traitors. They stood up for what was right, ended it all not with violence but intelligence, codes that stopped the killing, codes that have remained unbroken. I only wish I could have done more to help them when they were taken," said Carter with regret.

"I didn't know them." Maybe Sam was mad, mad that he never really knew them, mad that they had left too soon. He remembered adoring them and hating them, where yesterday he struggled to remember anything at all.

"It took courage to do what they did; it's a shame nobody else was like them, or the world would be a different place, a better place."

Sam didn't respond, it was all too much to take in and he was exhausted. Carter could tell that talk of his parents made him uncomfortable, but Jonathan and Elizabeth Royle were heroes and friends, and deserved more praise than the world gave them.

"Do you know why we went to so much trouble to bring you here?"

"No, and I doubt it will be worth the effort."

"Because you are special, you are a dreamer and the world needs you."

"A dreamer?"

"Your notepad: you dream, and you draw what you see. You can see the future even if you can't understand it."

Sam was too ill to remember anything. His notepad was a place of manic recordings, where he noted his time lapses and drew his visions. It was a product of illness, not premonition, and therefore this was impossible to believe.

"If I'm so special, then, why now?"

"Because our leader gave the order, our future requires it; political revolution, the Great House in ashes, our government gone, Union Front military on our streets, people taken in the night."

"Why me, why not someone else?"

"I'm afraid I had no choice in the matter."

"There's always a choice."

"Oh, Sam, if there was always a choice I wouldn't be here, and neither would you."

It hadn't yet dawned on him, the severity of the situation; there was something dark about this place and a prescient fear in Carter's eyes. The more he spoke, the more the charade of a nice old man dwindled.

"'You had the choice to leave me, the choice to not bring me here."

"Would you rather be left in that hellish place? Hooked on medication, weak and afraid?"

The issue made Sam uncomfortable. What if he was still trapped there? It seemed so far away now, and yet the thought made him speechless and he stepped back, aghast, until he collided with a cold metal wall. He turned in awe and saw something odd and irregular, a metal cube twelve feet long, tall and wide. An object so grand and vast, though with no clear purpose, that it stuck out like a sore thumb amongst the intricate counterparts that surrounded it. The cube was aged and rusted, weathered even, with a hatch on the side; underneath were signs of grass and dirt, as if it had been lifted from some unholy place and dropped here long ago.

"What is this?" asked Sam.

Carter moved closer to it, placing his hand on the metal.

"This – this is for another time."

Taken aback by the cube, Sam continued to stare. It lacked any sense, any logic; maybe that was what drew him to it.

Despite its unfamiliarity and Carter's spurious nature, Sam was getting used to this place until a red light shone down from a corner of the room. Sam flinched as it lit up. He looked at Carter, who seemed afraid; there was panic in the old man's eyes as he started looking around for something. He unpacked syringes, some of which were filled with a peculiar orange substance; his hands shook as he hurried around the room.

Sam watched the old man hobble, still tired and drowsy, his vision blurred, bringing a flashback of his headaches. He felt overwhelmed. The room had been so bright and white but now it seemed dark and claustrophobic.

"I need you to stay calm and do whatever they say."

Whatever they say? The thought echoed around Sam's mind, but he could not make any sense of it.

The stomping of boots interrupted his contemplation. Two guards entered by the glass door, emotionless and silent, wearing Union Front uniforms and armed with guns, grenades and stun batons; their boots thudded on the ground and their body language was less than friendly.

Sam was still in a daze, and he saw nothing but fear in Carter's eyes. Then he stared right at the soldiers, testing their patience. One had a scar across his cheek.

"Who is this?" the guard asked, stepping closer.

"He is the one we need," Carter replied, knowing that they couldn't risk such a vital Union asset. The guard looked Sam up and down and reached over his shoulder. He hit a button on the exoskeleton and it extended, sending Sam to the floor. As he fell, in the corner of his eye he could swear he saw a flash of green, a figure … but by the time he hit the ground it was gone.

Carter gasped, but both his hands remained in the air. He wanted to help Sam up but was too scared to do anything. His time in here had made him weak, a prisoner too damaged to fight or rebel; all he could do was work to keep his mind from failing.

"He is still weak, you fool," said Carter with some hesitation, but it was to no avail, the guards did not care.

"You have four subjects ready," he said.

"Please, we need more time. It needs further testing; we can't risk any more."

"Two are ready," the guard added with a complete lack of remorse.

"Please, twenty-seven have already been lost." Carter attempted to reason with them, but they were not here to reason, they had a job to do. One moved forward, gripping the frail old man by the collar.

"That's quite a record. I suggest improving or there may be no further use for you, do you understand?" He let go of Carter and gave a sick grin that told only of enjoyment.

"Yes, yes, I do," replied Carter as he hung his head.

"Good." The guard nodded, turned and walked away and the door shut behind them. Carter was distraught: so much hatred, so much death. He took a moment to pull himself together. Sam lay on the floor, coughing holding his gut, still weak from the machine, and angry that he could not summon the strength to act. He began to hyperventilate in shock before fighting off the panic attack.

"Breathe," said Carter, "breathe."

Carter reached for what seemed to be a respiratory mask and thrust it upon Sam's face; a few seconds later he was breathing normally again. Thoughts raced through his mind – the syringes, guards and conversation were enough to petrify him. Carter calmly lowered himself down and sat on the floor, but Sam shuffled backwards and pulled off the mask.

"Stay away from me, what have you done, why have you brought me here!"

"I'm sorry, Sam, it was the only way."

He was right to feel afraid; this place seemed worse than the city. Sam had a daunting realisation as the guards left that he was not free, that this was a prison. This whole place was locked down tight and no good could come from being here. It was all too much to process, though; the machine had messed with his mind and he was too weak to answer.

"What did they mean 'twenty-seven'?" Sam's question brought pain to Carter as he rested his head in his hands, afraid to speak.

"I … I am a monster. I have experimented on good people for the worst reasons … but I have no choice, Sam." He began to sob.

Sam listened to the old man wail; it was sad to see, and he placed a feeble hand on Carter's shoulder. "You gave me my mind back; no matter how bad this place is, I can live a better life."

"Do you think there is a God?"

"No, but I understand those that do."

"Do you think God would forgive me for what I have done? The lives I have taken here?"

Sam didn't want to answer; he had not thought of God in a long time and he was too tired, overcome with exhaustion.

"Twenty-seven have died by my hand, twenty-seven. When I first joined this programme, I thought we were doing this to change the world, to cure disease."

"Don't be so hard on yourself, it's clear you do not have a choice," replied Sam with a light cough, still holding his gut, which ached from the fall.

"Indeed, but I'm still a coward."

"You saved my life, and cowards don't save lives," Sam whispered faintly, overcome with exhaustion. He was as pale as a sheet, and the lights in here were bright and artificial; there was nothing natural about this place and he had already seen a ghost. Carter placed a hand on his forehead and then scanned him with some strange device. It bleeped and buzzed and then went quiet as a green light illuminated on its side. Then he reached over Sam's shoulder and pressed the same button as before; the suit kicked back into action and brought Sam to his feet, and slowly but surely Carter joined him.

"You need to rest. Here, let me show you the sleeping quarters." Sam struggled, even with the suit's help, but the doors opened and revealed a break room, with a small kitchen and a bunk bed, not much else. Carter ushered him to one of the bunks in a hurry and he lay down on his side. The suit retracted into a small handheld device; Carter took it and placed it in his pocket and then Sam was out like a light.

11

A LONELY ROAD

It was a gorgeous day in the park. The sun shone down and birds sang melodies of summer. Laughter filled the playground as children ran to and fro, enjoying the innocence of youth. Amongst them, a little girl with purple hair sat on a rusty red swing; she swung into the sky and back down again, forever aiming to fly. Kicking her legs back and forth to gain as much height as possible, higher and higher she pushed herself, and finally too far. For a moment she was weightless, but she fell to the ground hard, grazing her left knee and skidding along the ground, scratching her chin. She pulled herself up from the grey gravel and did not cry.

"Mama!" she shouted, but her parents were nowhere to be seen and black clouds blotted out the sun. Calling out again with no response, she felt alone and cold. She looked around to see the abandoned climbing frame, slides and swings. There was no one around, no one at all. The entire park was empty and as she pulled herself up there was silence all around.

Lydia lay in an alley between two high-rises, ten blocks lower than where she fell from. She came to in the alleyway – the suit had broken her fall. Lights shone around distant corners and the heavy chopping of a nearby helicopter split the air.

Come on, get up, Lydia said to herself. Sirens bellowed and beams shone down from far above. Stumbling, she tried to stand. In the corner of her eye was a sewer grating. Using the suit's strength, she pulled up the grating and crawled inside, closing the heavy lid behind her. Slipping from the ladder, she fell to the cold stone ground ten feet below – but the pain was nothing compared to the loss of her mother and father. The sound of his voice at the end was enough for her to know that they were gone.

Scrabbling around, she found a lighter in her pocket. She flicked it as her hands trembled, *scratch scratch scratch*, and finally there was light. The tunnels were never-ending, cold mossy brick walls filled with spiders, the squeaking of rats, and an awful odour. She moved as fast as possible, but her knee had taken a hard knock. Her breaths were heavy, as was her heart. Far from safety and all alone, with no choice but to keep going, she pushed on.

Her warm breath echoed off the walls and a shiver went down her spine. There was no hope but to move forward before catching a chill, following the downward flow, and hope that a river, an opening, anything, would be ahead.

Her head had taken a hard knock too, she couldn't feel her left arm and there was a piercing pain in her spine, but all this was as nothing compared to her father's last words. Only adrenaline and revenge kept her going. "*They will pay*," she said over and over.

The walk felt like forever, a cold stinking infinity with no way to tell how far she had gone. For hours Lydia wandered in darkness. Passage after passage, until she grew faint, her anger began to wear off and reality sank in.

They are gone, they are gone.

In the distance, the faint crashing of water brought her back. She picked up speed until the glimmer of hope inside her met with solid metal bars stopping her petite frame from passing through. Using the suit, she tried to pull the bars apart but the skeleton shuddered, low on power. With all her might she pleaded as she tried to pull the bars apart again, but they did not budge.

Banging her fists against them, she fell to the floor and screamed before she began to cry. She was tired, hungry and beyond thirsty. Lydia hadn't stopped moving since the phone call and she was covered in stinging cuts and bruises from her fall. The sewer's stench was also doing its work, and the darkness and claustrophobia setting in. The shock, the loss, the fall; it was too much to take in, yet she was not one to sit and feel sorry for herself, she had to push on.

Looking around, she saw no ladders or sewer grids to escape. The ground was cold, uneven, damp. It took any heat her legs had saved and drained it away. It hurt to stop, it meant thinking about her mother and father, how they were taken and how there was nowhere to go.

Yes, she was all alone now. Maybe this was where she should give up, give in.

What do I? she asked herself, as she would always ask her father. How she missed him, how he would hate to see her give in.

No, I will not give up. She looked around the old cold walls, a miracle that they were still standing. They were cracked and crumbling where the earth had moved them over time.

There was a faint white marking on the wall. Crawling towards it, she reached out and rubbed it with her fingers; it was not paint but chalk, and quite fresh. There she saw a crack in the rock, an opening. It was man-made, and the smallest glimmer of light shone in through the darkness. It looked tight but there seemed no other choice.

She began shimmying through; cobwebs brushed against her face, and something scurried over her feet. Her mind was filled with claustrophobic stress. Pulling herself along was easy at first but there seemed no end to the scratches, and each movement became heavy as the suit lost even more power. It was light as a feather when charged, but heavy as a ton of bricks when empty, and it was all out of juice – but it was all she had of him.

Her head became stuck against the rocks, then she was free again; the sharpness of the walls scraped her ears and elbows. The passage grew narrower until breathing was hard and she could only shuffle her feet. Fainting as the lack of breath took her, she saw a crack of hopeful light; but the path ahead was too tight.

This is it, she thought. *I push on and get stuck or turn back.*

After a few deep breaths – as deep as the walls would allow – she moved forward, pulling herself into the crevasse. For a moment or two Lydia could not breathe as she scraped against the walls, but then she was through.

Another section of sewer tunnels, another long dark passageway. But this time, at the end appeared a thick wooden door. An illusion, perhaps? As she got closer, she heard faint laughter.

Lydia hesitated; behind was only darkness, there was no going back. After a few seconds' contemplation, she booted the door and it opened into a dimly lit room. Sitting at a table were three surprised men, pistols next to each of them. In unison two stood and picked up their guns in shocked surprise.

"Who the hell are you?" one of them shouted. They looked at each other, confused, as Lydia stood panting, out of breath. She had been ready to fight, but the change in her surroundings, the odd sense of relief, made her faint, and she was out.

When she came to, things were fuzzy. Lydia realised she was being dragged through a large open storm drain. The eyes of men, women and children seemed to follow her every move between supplies stacked to the ceiling. She passed out again. A splash of cold water brought her back; she had awoken in a dark room. Ahead, a stranger leant against a raised platform, watching her. The room was stone but painted in wild colours, blues and yellows, to make it brighter; guards stood at her side, armed with machine guns and light weapons. They wore grey boots and trousers, and yellow sashes. Right away Lydia knew who they were.

"Leave us," one man shouted. His voice bellowed through the hall and the others were quick to leave.

"Drink?" he asked, throwing a large bottle of water in her direction. It tumbled, echoing, to the floor. Exhausted, Lydia scrambled to it. Snatching it up, she gulped it down before using it to wash away the dust and clean the scratches from the harsh walls. She wiped her face and took a moment to observe her surroundings: boxes of food and ammunition lay all around them. The figure opposite her was a large black man with a friendly smile; one of his eyes was glass, which glimmered in the candlelight; and he had a robotic hand that jittered. Its noise made it hard to concentrate.

"It's not often we have visitors, child. It was better you fainted, you got lucky. It gave me time to think things over instead of shooting first." His voice was deep and a strange mixture of Union, Kingdom and Cannon islands. He spoke in a deep slow voice and then paused, awaiting her reply, but none came.

"It's quite the suit you have there, some high-grade military shit. I could get good money for this."

She looked to her left and there was her suit, slumped like scrap metal. She felt naked without it.

"You wouldn't even know what to do with it," she returned.

"We would work it out, I'm sure; we worked out how to charge it," he said with a smile. "But where are my manners, I haven't even introduced myself."

"I know who you are, if the stories are true. The grave smuggler, Markus Vance."

Markus Vance was a legendary smuggler hailing from the south of the Union, having made a name for himself smuggling between the two great states and beyond. He moved everything from medical supplies to guns and ammunition, even luxury foods. It was said he would be worth millions if he didn't give it all away to feed the poor and fund his network of rebel militia. There was a high bounty on his head from either side, but no one would betray him and there were tall tales about how he could not die. Many said he was more machine than man on the inside; the many attempts to take his life had all failed. He was also an incredible negotiator; many said that he had the talent to get you to agree to anything. A colonel once came close to catching him and had him surrounded but was persuaded to leave his position to negotiate with him. Markus sent him back to his men cuffed behind his back with his pants down. From that day the colonel was known as Colonel Pants Down.

He let out a loud bellowing laugh as he leant back in his chair with a big open smile and slapped his thigh, but Lydia was not smiling. Markus loved underground fame and saw himself as a real-life Robin Hood.

"So, it appears the legend is real; do you know why they call us the grave smugglers?"

"You smuggled food and ammunition with bodies

in caskets during the war until your operation was rumbled."

The grave smugglers were no joke, they were said to be ruthless bandits. Markus nodded in acknowledgement; for such a dangerous man he had great charisma. He stood up and moved forward, folded his arms and stared down, his glass eye judging her.

"And what about you, I would have thought you were a special agent come here to take us down, but current affairs tell me something different. Hours ago, the Great House blew and the government that was afraid of me is gone, but my real enemies remain. I thought last night I would lose another outpost; the soldiers didn't come but they came for you, didn't they. Tell me why."

She took a minute and tried her best to judge him; it made her feel she had nothing to hide but she remained reserved and tough. He was playing nice, and she knew this face had a far more dangerous side; Markus was said to be a wicked man.

"I don't know what you're talking about," she replied – a blatant lie.

Markus raised an eyebrow with a smirk. He was not surprised, and expected her to be stubborn, but he did not expect her sadness.

"There was an explosion in an apartment on Fifth and they tried to take a girl, but this girl was highly trained, she wore a suit like yours."

She didn't say anything in response; no one could be trusted now, especially not a wanted man such as

Markus, not by a soldier … but then she was a soldier no more.

"If you know who I am and I know who you are, why haven't you killed me?"

Markus's hand twitched and jerked; defective, it never stopped moving; upon meeting him it was hard to concentrate on anything else. He raised it and held his chin to halt its movement.

"I don't kill for sport; I don't kill for pleasure, those we kill have what we want or want to kill us."

"What about me?"

"What about you indeed. You are alive because you could be useful." He stood with his hands behind his back. "Take a walk with me," he said.

She wanted to do nothing; the pain was deep and one that only revenge could cure; yet she pulled herself up and took one last look at her suit, then followed.

They passed the guards and for a moment Lydia thought about grabbing a gun from one of them, take a few down – but without the suit, escape would not be possible.

The storm drain was vast. Man-made shacks lined the walls, bunks hung from odd pipes, and supplies were stacked high. It was an underground town full of strange wonders, shacks, stalls and private quarters. Several fire pits, too; one had a roasted pig rotating over it. The smell was sweet. There were many tables, and people everywhere in rags and blankets, staring afar. Many turned away as she looked, suddenly growing quiet.

It dawned on her that this so-called anti-statist

terrorist was not the wicked man she had been led to believe. Here was his colony, his people; he provided for them and gave them safety from the cruel realities above.

"I thought you a soldier?"

"I'm a realist, and the world I build is real. We have food and medicine; contraband from the world above. We have doctors and nurses, teachers and builders, yet never enough soldiers."

Markus glanced towards a teenager who walked past, as young as fourteen. He carried a machine gun on his shoulder that was much too big for him. Markus messed up his hair and smiled.

"Atilla! How are your mother and sister?"

"Ahh, can't complain," he replied with a buck-toothed grin.

Atilla shot a sharp glance at Lydia before walking towards one of the guard towers looming over them.

"You are giving children guns?" Lydia asked in shock.

"The children of the dead want to fight."

She looked around at all the faces, and distasteful stares followed her every move. Some frowned, others scowled, and some ignored her. It appeared that wherever they walked, the people grew silent.

"Why do they stare with such cold eyes?" she asked.

"Word travels fast, they know who you are, what you have done."

He was right about what had she done. Her brethren had destroyed outposts and killed innocent people, while the establishment and the media painted a picture of glory and safety. Riots were crushed, people disappeared, and things were only getting worse; what kept them in line was fear, but even that was dying.

"No one knows anything about me."

"You would be surprised at what can be inferred from looking at the face of a soldier. They are good people and can warm to outsiders, but not those with dog tags."

Markus pointed at the tags hanging around her neck; she had forgotten about them and covered them now with her hand, held them tight, and remembered she wore both hers and her father's. Given to her when he retired, she would never take them off, not now, not ever.

"I was told you were animals, cold-blooded killers."

"You were lied to, like most on the surface," replied Markus with another smile. He noticed she kept looking past him at something. He turned around and saw the roasting hog twisting and smoking in the flames, with baked apples all around.

"Hungry?" Markus asked. Lydia nodded, and they walked over to the roast. A dirty chef stood turning the pork, his belly bulging underneath the grease-covered apron he wore.

"Gary, this one smells beautiful," Markus said, sniffing the hog and giving its rear end a polite tap in jest.

"Thank you, sir, fresh from the Prime Minister's estate. After the raids the whole place was abandoned; we got four pigs, eight hens and two cows," replied Gary, wiping his hands on his apron.

"Cut a piece for our guest, please," said Markus, so Gary cut a large juicy slab of pork, slathered fresh bread with butter and served a heap of juicy stuffing. Markus passed the plate and Lydia's eyes lit up.

"Come sit," he said, pointing at the nearest empty table. They sat down and she did not hesitate to dig in, devouring the soft, sweet-smelling pork with no patience or courtesy. Before she finished, little footsteps pattered toward the table, the sound of a small child.

"Markus! Markus! I made you a drawing!" A little girl of about six approached the table. Markus stood up and lifted her into the air, spinning her in circles before placing her back down.

"Eliza! You get bigger every time I see you!"

Markus picked up the drawing and looked at the stick-man in crayon.

"It's you!" said the sweet little girl.

"It looks just like me, little one. Now run home and show this to your mother."

It hit her then most of all, when she saw the little girl with such hopeful eyes, so happy at the simplicity of her drawing. She could not help but see herself and think of times long gone. Showing her own father her drawings after waiting for him to get home from work felt like yesterday. Things were much simpler as a child, no matter how cruel the world around them had been even then.

"Sorry about that," said Markus, trying to look tough as he took his seat.

"Is that your daughter?"

"No, but they are all my children, one and the same."

A little bit more of what she thought she knew about Markus Vance and the grave smugglers faded away. It became clear that he was a man of the people and that those Robin Hood stories might be true – but still he was a wanted man.

Markus leant in with his arms folded; he looked her up and down for a moment as she finished her plate.

"Do you know why they blew up the Great Houses?" he asked – a straightforward question, but one with a complicated answer.

"My father wouldn't," she replied in defence, pushing the plate away from her. Markus tilted his head and observed her reaction.

"I'm not accusing, I'm asking. *Why* would generals rise against their state? It makes no sense to me." Trying to understand, he picked his teeth and awaited her answer.

"It was Sahl, he killed them all." Her tone was stern and full of hatred; just saying his name brought the idea of revenge. Markus took one look into her eyes and knew too well the pain and hate she bore; he had seen it many times before. His usual smirk disappeared at the mention of that name.

"Nathan Sahl … A man painted the hero is sometimes the villain."

The truth began to dawn on Markus.

"So Sahl murdered the government and made the people welcome Union soldiers to our shores."

Markus's metal hand made a fist on the table.

"But why?" he asked.

"I don't know, but what I do know is that he will die, mark my words."

Markus seemed not to react to her threat, he seemed detached from it, as if not fully comprehending how serious she was. He began to play with the three coins in his hand as Lydia watched.

"The longer you play the game, the longer you stop focusing on what you can see, sometimes it's best to step back and take a long look at what you might be missing."

Markus revealed his hand to show only two coins, and then he opened his other hand to reveal the third before giving his famous smile.

"I don't have time for games, I'm going to kill him," Lydia insisted.

"Many have tried, and many have died."

"You think I can't do it?" There was a sharpness to her voice.

"If you are going to kill Nathan Sahl, you should kill every soldier that has put on Union uniform, and finally the Union Council. There is much more at play than one man – can you kill them all?"

"It may take me my entire life, but I will die trying."

"Not on your own." Markus crossed his arms and shook his head.

Despite her stubborn nature, she knew he was right; it could not be done alone but by God she would die trying if she had to.

"You can help me?"

Markus placed the metal hand on his rough chin in

a fine thinking pose and glanced at those who needed him now more than ever.

"Right now, I have a hundred people in my care. I need every able soldier protecting the outposts and our people. I could do with someone with your training and expertise."

It hit her that she was alive because he wanted something. But as quaint as this place was, she could not consider his offer; her one-track mind had one goal, revenge. Anything else was futile.

"I'm afraid I can't," she replied. Markus wasn't pleased.

"And why is that?"

"I must keep going until he is dead."

"There isn't a day that goes by when I don't think of him. Sahl is my curse too. For too long his crimes have gone unanswered and now the stomping boots of foreign soldiers plague my city. We don't have the fire-power and I can't risk my people."

"You are afraid."

"No, Markus Vance is never afraid, but he is no fool."

Markus lost himself for a second in anger where before he had been calm and diplomatic. Lydia was tired and angry and would stop at nothing until she had revenge.

"I can't give you what you want but I can give you something better," Markus replied.

"What?" She could see her own reflection in his glass eye as he moved around the table.

"The chance to build something, something better."
A hopeful grin followed his words.

"I'm no Samaritan."

"I'm not asking for a Samaritan, only a soldier."

"No," she insisted.

"Why not?"

"I am better off alone."

"Aren't we all, yet fate brought us together."

She was in no mood to be a hero or a martyr.

"Just give me my suit so I can leave, I have bigger things to do."

"Look around you, look at these people. They need your help. *I* need your help." His tone had changed, showing a softer side to him; she couldn't help but listen despite her drive to go.

"I can't stay."

"Just one job … I need you and your expertise. There is a temporary Union base called Nexa, have you heard of it?"

"I'm sorry," she said with regret, shaking her head.

"Very well." Markus whistled and one of his men came and handed him the suit. He looked down, admiring its craftsmanship before handing it over. It was heavy but he made light work of it; she latched onto it and stepped away.

"Go on your journey alone, then. I wish you good fortune, but it only ends one way." He raised his robotic hand and pointed down a corridor. "That is the way out." He turned and pointed the other way. "If you ever come back, the second door there is where you will find me."

She looked in both directions, gave a nod and walked towards the exit, alone again. Markus didn't say goodbye, but he did watch her walk away before making his way into a corridor. He opened the second door, to a room where two men played cards, and took a seat next to them.

"You were always terrible with women, brother," one of them said before breaking into a fit of laughter. His name was Gabriel. He was as tall but far slimmer, faster, and considered himself to be funnier than Markus, although he was not as bright. Gabriel had been his brother's right-hand man since the beginning and he too was considered unkillable. The Union army once had his base of operations surrounded and he walked out in Union uniform right past Colonel Pants Down. He also claims to hold the record for the longest sniper shot in history, nearly four thousand metres.

"Much better than you, even with this eye!" Markus was quick to reply, and Gabriel howled with laughter. The other man was a big hairy giant with a large beard and a bald head. Youssef was his name – Youssef the Bear. He had met the Vance brothers as part of a wager, whereby Markus had drunkenly claimed he could defeat any man hand-to-hand in Reach's capital city, Labore. He did not expect one of those men to be the undefeated Union military bare-knuckle boxing champion. Youssef had been exiled and spoke little English, but that didn't matter. He spoke with his fists when needed, but was otherwise a teddy bear. He was chewing a toothpick whilst trying to make sense of the playing cards in front of him.

"It was a no, then?" said Gabriel, not looking away from the cards.

"I'm afraid it was; it's a shame, she could have been useful," said Markus, "but let's not hang our heads yet …"

Gabriel gave a sigh before finally placing his cards down. Then the door creaked open and to everyone's surprise Lydia stood awkwardly in the darkness of the threshold.

"I've been to Nexa," she said before stepping inside and pulling up a chair as Markus gave a smile.

"Sit down," he ushered. "This is Gabriel, and Youssef." He tossed her a beer, she caught it mid-air and slammed it down on the edge of the table, leaving the bottle cap to rattle on the floor. Gabriel kept his hand over the cards and gave a polite nod. Lydia looked up at Youssef, who sat on a chair far too small him, that creaked beneath him.

"How do," he said in a deep bass tone.

Markus unrolled a few sheets, blueprints of the sewer system, and pushed the playing cards out of the way. Lydia saw a vast maze of tunnels, some she must have passed through herself.

"Have you done a job like this before?" asked Youssef in his gruff, broken voice. Lydia looked up at him and almost gave a smile, if only for revenge.

"What do you know about Nexa?" Gabriel asked.

"I know it was closed for years. If it's back up and running, it will be a station for Union Front soldiers. I know a way in, I know where the trucks will be and I know those fences are weak," she said, taking a swig.

She picked up a pack of cigarettes without asking and pulled one out, lighting it with the lucky flame that got her through the tunnel.

"We leave at midnight, then. Make sure you read the sewer plans," said Markus as he threw the diagrams in her direction. The original plans had been drawn over, having been frequently changed. The grave smugglers closed certain pathways and opened new ones, which allowed them to control large territories from underground.

"So, we have two hours to kill before show time," she said, looking forward to the excitement of a gunfight.

Youssef stood up. "Girl," he said, which stopped her in her tracks. "What is your name?"

"My name was Captain Lydia Jacobs, but just call me Lydia."

12

THE REASONS WHY

He was Vincent once, and for most of his life, to loved ones and friends. Younger then, confident, inventive and inspiring, now he was old and afraid. Alone but for his work. Now his name was Doctor Carter and he saw no friends or loved ones anymore; they were lost long ago. Carter shuffled, slow and solemn, with a syringe bag in hand and his head down, staring at the ground, through automatic glass doors. His welcoming persona was left farther behind with every step as he moved on to something much darker.

Guards flanked him down the long corridors, watching his every move in silence; they had nothing to say and neither did Carter. He knew where he was going: section nine. He knew what awaited him, and why. It was an awful place, one of pain and sadness, and though he left often, it never left his mind. In section nine, his morals sank away past the dark heavy doors. It was a damp, concrete place more run-down than the last, as every expense was indeed spared. Empty hospital beds and a stale smell of metal stained the air, but Carter had grown used to it. He walked past a cold concrete room and looked inside. Its glass was one-way so no one within could see out, and even if they could they would have seen only a shameful old man with a clipboard noting their deformities, watching their humanity decompose and wither away with his own.

That room was for the patients, those who became subjects. Here they would huddle cold and dying as their minds gave up, always before their bodies. Many came in, but none had ever left. It was the end of a line and not a fine end at that. Carter could tell that its purpose was coming to an end itself; it had been weeks since they had brought in any new specimens. Something was happening above, for sure, but he had no way of knowing what it was.

Carter entered the final room, where hospital beds stood in rows accompanied by heavy restraints. Of the twelve beds set out in rows of three, only two were taken and in those beds lay two male subjects, strapped down, already dosed. A numbing agent was used to stop them from speaking, but they were conscious, and panic could be seen within their eyes. Carter found the muffled moans they made much worse than their screams. Screaming was a human instinct, a combative response, where a dosed-up plea, a moan, was an unnatural, desperate noise.

The subjects lay still, unable to move as much as they wanted to. Carter shuffled around the nightmare as if stalling for time, but he remembered the presence of the guards, the beatings, the threats and everything else that came before. Carter held a needle in one hand, filled with a viscous orange substance. He looked around and saw two guards watching him through a window, batons in hand. He injected the first subject, hating himself as he did; *It's going to be alright*, he wanted to say aloud whilst staring into the teary eyes of his first today. The subject's eyes were dazed but a soul was still in there, staring back at him.

The serum met his bloodstream and the veins around the wound began to swell as the man burst into life. He wrestled to free himself as the medication wore off instantly; he roared and tumbled back and forth shaking under heavy restraints. Carter knew this reaction would not last long, so he turned to the second man, who was more alive within the eyes. He stared right back at Carter with more awareness than the other. Carter could see the fear and the pain, the plea, but he knew there was no choice. He sank a fresh syringe into the man's arm whilst looking away. *It will be over soon*, Carter told himself once more.

The two men began to shake and tried to scream; they swelled up, muscles growing, veins pushing to the surface. Dripping with sweat, they attempted to fight the fever, but it was too much. Vomit flew from their mouths, blood from their ears, as they struggled, resisting violently. They were bigger now, much bigger, and bright red, as their blood tried to deal with the pain and the power. The eyes of one were about to pop; he lifted his chest far away from the bed, then fell back down as his heart stopped.

The other grew so warm that his face was a shade of

purple. Hyperventilating with a heavy, wheezing chest, white foam dribbled from his mouth. Carter looked into his eyes with a feeble sense of shame and waited, praying for him to pass. The specimen had overstayed his time, but now, against all odds, he turned a shade of grey as the effects of the serum quietened down. Struggling against his restraints, he ripped one hand free with tremendous strength and went for Carter's throat. One small squeeze of the old man's frail neck would end him. Carter didn't retreat; he moved forward to let the monstrous creation grab him, in the hope of what he deserved. As he stared into the eyes of his end, as quickly as the specimen had tried to grasp him, he let go and slumped back lifeless, while Carter hit the floor.

Carter pulled himself up using the side of the bed, feeling far too old for such horrors, and tried to catch his breath. It would have been a quick end, quicker than most, but he knew deep down it was not the way he would go. Carter was cursed with having foreseen his own death, and he'd wished many times that it would come sooner, but it could not.

He gave a traditional moment's silence for those lives lost. He wondered who they were, the stories they shared, whether they had children, wives, passions. In the full force of his shame, a slow and sarcastic round of applause came from behind to interrupt him: *clap, clap, clap.* Upon realising who it was, Carter felt terror, and then he buried that feeling deep, for, as much as he didn't want to, he had to turn to face his demon. It took the form of a tall, slim, aged woman in a lab coat. She stood at the end of the bed with a sickly smile, sharp features, teeth too white, and dark eyes that held a hint of madness, eyes that stared too long and didn't blink enough. Her presence left Carter with only one instinct: to cower away.

"Another failure – you don't fool me; you weren't close at all. None of your patients has ever come close." Carter shuddered at the sound of her voice; there was an irate haughtiness to it that pierced the air.

"Doctor Monroe, I-I-I didn't know that you would be coming here yourself." Carter was caught off guard; he got himself to his feet, wary and hesitant.

"I shouldn't need to be here. We've grown tired of your mistakes, you have failed us, you and your feeble excuses."

"But I'm so close, I –"

"We think it may be time you *retired*."

Monroe didn't have a way with words, but one word, *retirement*, echoed around Carter's mind. Here such a term had another meaning. It meant death, and he had been fearful of it for too long. But he was conditioned, institutionalised, and fought to please, through the fear. He had grown used to the reality that he would never see his family again; after all, he had traded his life for theirs. Here he was, far from them, deep underground, away from daylight, nature and beauty, trembling at the will of those who were once considered colleagues.

"You need me," he replied without thinking, his first instinct being to play the pathetic card of the pleaser. As much as he did not wish to beg or be a coward, captivity made it instinctive.

"Need you? We are tired of you and we have tolerated your failure for far too long." Her bitter digs didn't seem to scar him in the same way anymore. Monroe was the sort of person who enjoyed belittling someone lower down the ladder, but she didn't taste the same satisfaction with him. "You always look as if there is some sort of joke going on that I am not a part of, Carter."

"I don't know what you mean."

"I think you do," Monroe snapped. To her he was a failure, but his subjects had shared a quicker death than through the eternal servitude intended for them, and this was Carter's intention. That was his joke, his way to get back at them, to show that they didn't always win even if they didn't know it. He spiked the syringes with chemicals to put his subjects out of their misery. Though playing the part of a feeble coward, he would rather die than let any of their experiments work. Playing God was not a game Carter wished to be a part of. He knew it was only a matter of time before his plan was discovered – that he had taken the lives of those in front of him to save them from a fate worse than death. He was not ashamed but damn well proud of it and was happy to have got away with it for as long as he had. So he lifted his chin high, as if for the first time.

"No one deserves the life you put in front of them, even death is better," said Carter in an honest voice, one of newfound pride.

"Did I just hear your spine grow a little? Maybe you have forgotten your place. You have compromised years of research, you conniving little worm; you have accomplished *nothing*."

His patience was wearing thin; he was polite and courteous at the most challenging of times, but Carter had been pushed too far. All it took was a spark, and in this cold and lonely place one spark could go a long way. It was so easy to slip into madness, and Monroe was begging for it. Carter raised a fist and brought it down through a glass vial, shattering it as he did.

"Haven't I done enough?" he shouted, puffing and panting, too old and tired for this.

"No, not enough."

"What more do you want from me, what more can I possibly give?" His anger was rife; it was unlike him to lose it, but this had gone too far.

"Don't you dare take such a tone with me, your charade has gone on long enough, you are a disgrace to us."

"Us? You and your pathetic regime – your leader can –"

"Our leader can what?" came a rough, familiar voice from behind him. Carter had not seen or heard him enter the room; the man moved like a ghost when he wanted to. Carter didn't know how long he had been standing there but he now turned around to see his combat vest, his long coat and leather gloves. Nathan looked intimidating and stood clasping something in his hand. It was a puzzle cube, faded with age, and Carter's eyes locked on to it.

"Nathan I, I didn't know you were here," said Monroe hanging her head. Carter could not speak; he had lost all confidence at the sight of the cube; it had hit him with memories of childhood: a gift he had passed on to his son was now in Nathan's hands.

"I was told this is to go to your grandchild. I trust your son will want to pass on your methods. Don't worry," said Nathan, tossing the cube into the air and catching it again, "they are still well looked after." Carter stared down at the cube; there was a faint glimmer of hope in his eyes at the mention of his life outside this place, before it disappeared again.

"I didn't mean what I said. I —" Carter back-tracked, unsure of what to say or do. Nathan leant on one of the beds and avoided looking at either of the corpses. He was in a peculiar mood. It was always hard to tell what he was thinking, and now it was harder than ever, given the burden upon his shoulders.

"I don't need you to lie to me, Carter, that's not what I need from you."

"Well, what do you need?"

"The Great Houses are gone, the Ministry is gone, and all my enemies are gone." Carter's throat was dry as he tried to swallow. He had hoped and prayed for many things over the years and the Kingdom government's intervention to close this cruel place was one of them, but he didn't understand the betrayal of the Ministry. "I need the Titan online in two days."

"It isn't possible; Sam's too weak. We haven't the time, it's a huge leap to assume that he could lead us to the answer in two days."

"Strange, considering it was your idea to bring him back from the brink," Monroe butted in as Carter looked at each of them, back and forth. He tried to stay calm, but promising that Sam would be the one to turn on the Titan was always a shot in the dark.

"Well, if you want me to do it, I need more information. Why Sam?" asked Carter, unsure of his plan.

"Samuel Royle's parents built the Titan's safeguarding mechanism. His memories hold the key to turning it on."

It made sense to Carter as he began to piece everything together; he had known Sam was important, although not for this. There was irony in Nathan's words; Sam's memories had been wiped for a different reason and now the very man that was involved in their vanishing wanted them restored.

"If that is true, then his parents, Jonathan and Elizabeth, would have hidden it well. It may take months to find."

"You don't have months." Monroe spoke sharply.

"I didn't ask you to contribute," said Nathan raising his hand, and Monroe went silent. He was the only person in the world she would be silent for: Nathan had saved her life when she was still a combat medic and she would forever be in his debt. Nathan turned to Carter once more and looked him up and down. "The Ministry of Men wanted you terminated, to be buried down here with all your secrets. None of this is what I wanted, but I am involved all the same. I know you are a good man and I want you to go home to your family. Find the solution, Carter, get it done."

Carter nodded with a look of defeat; he would never trust any of them, but he was smart enough to do as they said. He had maintained the same expression with

Monroe and the guards for years. Nathan stepped forward and walked towards him, coming too close for comfort. He took Carter's hand as it flinched, and placed the cube within it. Carter grasped it tight, put the cube in his pocket and began to pack his syringes.

"And Carter."

"Yes?" he asked, stopping still.

"We need more vials of the serum – one last extraction, for the Titan."

Carter froze and said nothing, then he gasped as thoughts raced through his mind. This was his death sentence; if they left for the Titan, he would surely not go with them.

"Of course," he muttered, finally summoning the courage to respond.

Nathan turned and walked away as two guards escorted him through doors that Carter could never have passed through himself. Monroe did not so much as blink, and despite how much he wanted her to go she continued to watch his every move.

"Good luck, Carter," she said, and went to take her leave before pausing at the door. "Oh, and Carter, clean this place up, it smells of your mistakes."

The room was quiet, the smell of his experiments foul. Thoughts continued to race through his mind; he was sick of this painful existence, but in his pocket he grasped the cube tightly, for it brought him hope.

13

REMEMBER THEM

The streets were quiet, in mourning. Nathan and Rose sat silently in the back of their limousine. Today was a dark day for her, while for him it was supposed to be the most important day of his life. He knew the Union would be watching, that unlike other days today would go down in history, but he felt a terrific sense of shame. There was a weight massing upon his shoulders for every deed done since becoming Chief and giving the order, and he began to fear it might never lift.

The road to the funeral was long at such slow speed. Rose had not grown used to the military convoy – she had not grown used to many things. The funeral was to be held across from the smouldering ashes of the Great Houses, in the cathedral. It was as close as Nathan had been since the blaze, and he was aware that the Great Houses' embers were still fresh and smoking. How he hated that smell, and how impossible it was to remove it from his clothes.

Nathan looked down, fearing the world he had created beyond the windows. He felt tired; the once charming man looking back at him was fading with the loss of good friends. He looked back at Rose, who was dressed all in black. She was pale and in tears, as she had been since hearing the news. Nathan felt their bump, held her hand and gave a reassuring smile, but it didn't seem worth anything.

"Is something wrong?" he asked with deep concern, lifting her sunken chin.

"I-I'm fine, I just have a headache, that's all." Something had been bothering her all morning, but she did not wish to worry him, not today. It was hard for her, as the cameras flashed away; Rose had never been one to adore the spotlight, she hated cameras and publicity.

There was no traffic on the main roads; even the buses had been called to a halt. The only vehicles were ones taking bankers, bureaucrats and philanthropists to the funeral. Everything seemed tranquil, but they soon came upon the first roadblock, then another, and another. At each one Rose saw the Union uniforms, black and white, bearing the insignia of the Crane; it dawned on her how quickly the world had changed in such a short time. Too often had she turned a blind eye to everything, but now that Evelyn was gone it was all too real.

At each checkpoint were a number of detainees, prisoners looking skinny and browbeaten. Rose couldn't help but look at them where Nathan looked away. She watched a Union guard beat a man to the ground with the butt of his rifle.

"Stop!" she shouted, and the limousine came to a halt. Rose opened the door and stumbled over to the men as the Union guards raised their guns at her. "Don't hurt him, leave him alone," she said, out of breath but desperate to do what Evelyn would have done. Nathan grabbed her from behind and the soldiers lowered their weapons. Rose screamed and fought to no avail as Nathan desperately tried to get her to hold it together. After a while he managed to escort her back to the limousine, and just like that it was as if nothing had happened. No pictures were taken to document the scene; it was a serious offence for photographers to take pictures demeaning the state.

Similarly, the culling of those who opposed Nathan went untelevised. The rioters' voice was quashed entirely. Today's news gave the illusion of a nation coming together. The crowds gathered appearing to want to pay their respects following the burning of the Great Houses – but there had been promises of additional rations for those who showed. It was the strangest image, as hundreds of impoverished people who had gone through hell stood in silence together. They didn't cry or cheer or show any emotion at all; instead they just stood waiting.

As Nathan and Rose approached the cathedral and the limousine came to a halt it was easy to see that the people were not simply upset but defeated. A member of the Union guard opened the door upon their arrival, and hand in hand they walked the hundred metres down the Great Road to the cathedral as photographers with wide smiles took sanctioned photographs. A full choir accompanied the scene, echoing from the cathedral's open doors, and every step was difficult for Rose. The world she had woken up to seemed a charade – although maybe it always was that way, and she had not taken enough notice to see it. Still she held Nathan's hand tightly; if she didn't, she might faint.

Red, white and blue flowers, flags and banners in Kingdom's colours covered the Great Road, separating Nathan and Rose from the hundreds of miserable onlookers and the lines of Union guards. The people did not shout or curse. They were silent, lost in the choir's hypnotic melodies.

Nathan gave a few nods and waves as they walked up the steps. The public news channel was making him out to be a hero who had ended tyranny in one night, yet he did not feel like a hero, not today. At the top of the steps, at the huge arching entrance of aged sandy stone, Nathan turned to Rose and gave her a polite kiss before they entered through the great oak doors. Hundreds sat in pews facing the front row, the most celebrated names in Sovereign. In the front row were the loved ones of the lost, filled with a false sense of hope by Nathan. They did not know the truth and never would.

At the front, twelve elegant coffins lay covered with flowers. Seeing them, the guards, the crowd, it all hit Rose; Nathan had kept her out of the public eye for so long that she didn't know where to look. He held her hand to make her feel better; hers was very cold. She found it hard to stay focused, to concentrate on anything but the sadness and the nerves.

Nathan noticed that Drake's seat was empty – something was wrong. Surveying the crowd, a terrifying mixture of emotions consumed him for what he had done; he sat back and tried to put it out of his mind and let the peaceful choir take over. He closed his eyes and listened to their voices, hymns he had heard before in a different church, one that he had visited many times, one that he had asked forgiveness in too often. When the songs of prayer came to an end, the priest took to the pulpit; he looked uncomfortable and unwilling, but it was his duty to speak. He reminded Nathan of the priest who had listened to his confession, the priest who had died. All of a sudden Nathan couldn't get him out of his mind; it was as if he were watching, looking down and judging him.

"Dearly beloved, we gather here today to celebrate the lives of those who have left us. Those who risked their lives to bring peace and order to our nation in its time of need; those who stood in courage at a time when many failed. They understood the risks in what they faced, but stood in the eye of the storm making decisions to try and save our great nation. It is in such desperate times that we must face such fear with love, where we must embrace each other and remember our heroes. I bless those who left us, in the name of the fathers, the mothers and the Union. May their sacrifice bring us better days, for we must move forward. We thank those who have stepped up to continue such great work."

Nathan stopped listening; he held Rose's hand and just wanted this whole thing to be over. He looked out upon the crowd and felt a great sense of unease; the sobs of those who had lost their loved ones were all he could hear.

"… and now I ask our right honourable Chief of Defence, Nathan Sahl, to speak."

The priest's words were met with a short, shallow round of applause, and then the room fell silent. Rose squeezed his hand so tightly it brought him back as everyone stared on. Nathan wanted to stand but couldn't for a moment; Rose squeezed his hand again. Nathan stood and adjusted his jacket nervously; public speaking wasn't something he did often, although he had a knack for it. Approaching the podium slowly, he placed both hands upon it; he had anticipated this moment for a long time, standing before his people unopposed. No more slander, no one talking down to him. He looked around for a moment or two, then down at his crumpled piece of paper and then to the front row, where he saw something haunting.

Sitting in front of him, struggling to sit up with his arms folded, was the priest, with bruises on his neck and bulging eyes. Next along were Carl and Debbie Jacobs, a bag upon her head and tyre marks across Carl's chest. Every member of the cabinet, too – Davies, Miles – and every general. Baylor himself. Even Doctor Carter, shrunken and hunched. Cat, the Union spy was there admiring her killer claws, Rogan the Union Council's leader, and last of all – last of all, Sam. Nathan's mouth was very dry, and it burnt to blink his eyes. Trembling as he opened his bottle of water, he took a cold swig.

On glancing back, they were all gone, but he could feel the priest still watching.

"I can't describe to you my deep sorrow," he mumbled before clearing his throat. "I can't describe to you how awful I felt when I received the news that our beloved leaders had been taken from us, one of whom was a close personal friend. It saddens me to see our country in such turmoil, in such pain, and it has been hurting for the longest time." He paused to take a breath and looked over at Rose.

"We won't let this day be forgotten or let our heroes be forgotten. Together we can make everything better. With new life comes a bright future …"

Nathan paused for a moment as a man staggered down the middle aisle, veering from one side to the other. It was Drake, drunk or worse. Nathan tried to concentrate on the task at hand, but it became impossible as Drake's footsteps echoed, breaking his trail of thought.

"We … we can … We can all …"

Nathan halted on seeing the dark black lines under Drake's eyes. Drake went past his seat to Evelyn's coffin and stood there like a ghost. Placing a hand on the smooth shining wood, Drake stared deep into Nathan's soul.

"So, this is how you sell it to them, your master plan." Drake's voice echoed through the tall cathedral and everything stopped. A guard moved slightly toward him, but Nathan met him with such a stare that the rest remained perfectly still. The loved ones of those lost looked puzzled as they gazed upon the dishevelled figure of Drake Owen. Drake moved towards the staircase and climbed up; armed guards moved in before being signalled to stop. Drake stood opposite Nathan, centre stage, his dark-eyed stare making Nathan feel even more guilty.

What are you doing, you fool! Nathan thought to himself.

"What if I told you, the people, that this man is a liar, that he will do whatever it takes to betray you. He would stab you in the back and take everything from you. All of this was his doing!"

The television broadcast ceased, the screens outside facing the crowd went blank, but Drake had already awoken their rage. The crowd began throwing bottles and anything else to hand. People chanted and booed, remembering how things had been yesterday. As Nathan and Drake faced each other on the stage, armed guards awaited the signal to take Drake down, but Nathan wouldn't give it. There was a tremendous tension between them, broken only by Drake producing the gun Nathan had given him. His hand was shaking as the silence between them dragged on.

"Please, Drake, put it down, please," begged Rose. She could not breathe, she was faint, nauseous and overcome by pain. Lunging forward, she fell to her knees, wanting to vomit, but nothing came out. Drake glanced at her for a second and then turned back to his enemy. Rose only reminded him of Evelyn and the sorrow that brought; she did nothing to make him want to relinquish the weapon.

"You don't know him, Rose, you don't really know him," said Drake.

"Please, just put it down," she repeated, clutching her swollen belly and groaning. Drake dried his eyes with one sleeve before raising it high once more.

"I loved you like a brother and you killed her, you fucking killed her," he whimpered with a crazed look in his eye as Nathan continued to hold both his hands in the air.

"Drake, I –"

Drake fired three shots; people screamed, hid behind pews and tried to scatter. Armed guards ran forward and tackled Drake as to his dismay Nathan stood unharmed, staring down at him with a ravenous vengeance.

It was chaos as the congregation ran towards the doors and Union guards blocked the exit. Things were growing worse outside the building, too. The crowd that had given such welcome grew even more restless at the sound of gunshots. More bottles were thrown, and when some of the crowd tried to break the lines and move towards the church, the guards opened fire. A mass of screaming followed as they fell one by one. The rest scattered, running in every direction to escape the carnage.

Inside, the guards formed a barrier at the door to stop those inside from leaving.

"Order! Stand back! I won't tell you again!" one of the Union guards shouted, and the panic in the church turned to silence. Nathan cast around desperately, disoriented by the deafening shots; everything appeared to be crashing down around him. He could tell by the faces of those inside the cathedral that they held no adoration for him – a few words from an honest friend had ruined everything. His name had been tarnished, and he knew that the Council was watching.

He climbed to his feet and saw Drake being hand-cuffed and beaten. Nathan gazed over at Rose. She had collapsed and was lying on the floor. Nathan ran over to her.

"Rose, stay with me. Is there a doctor here?" Nathan looked at the timid crowd trapped in silent fear ahead of him. A man in funereal black raised his hand and was led up the stairwell amidst the commotion. He made an assessment and looked up at Nathan with a sense of uncertainty. "She's breathing, but she needs to go to hospital, there's nothing anyone can do from here."

"Take her to the Sovereign Central … Caleb, instruct them to clear the entire fourth floor and secure the perimeter."

Caleb placed a reassuring arm on Nathan's shoulder and nodded, then he signalled his men to move out. Rose was placed on a stretcher and carried through the back door.

"What about this terrorist, sir?" said one of the guards pushing Drake to the floor as his eyes stared with a mix of fear and anger.

"Put him in a van. I will speak with him when I'm ready."

After dealing with Drake, Nathan instructed the soldiers to make way for Rose. The crowd remained seated, shaken, waiting for things to die down outside;

there was gunfire in the distance, and it made them very afraid. With every spray of bullets, they ducked as the sound echoed through the nave of the cathedral. Holes punctured the stained-glass as shards fell down and those below took cover. They waited with watchful eyes whilst the chaos continued inside and out, until finally being allowed to leave.

Nathan was quiet and stern. He hid his emotions well, but his fear for Rose overwhelmed him. He tried to clear his throat and place his worries at the back of his mind. He stood still on the stage despite Rose and Drake being carried off elsewhere and the cathedral emptying around him. He thought of how different this day should have been, how all he wanted to do was protect those he loved, friends and family. There was no going back, not from the decision he had made. Nathan took his time leaving the building by the back door, where a small force of soldiers awaited him. As he passed through the security line and various trucks, he reached a large white van with two guards standing beside it.

"We roughed him up good and proper, sir, you –"

"Leave," said Nathan, and the two guards walked away from the venomous look in his eyes. Nathan opened the van door and climbed inside. He saw Drake sitting on his knees, his hands tied behind his back. There was a small pool of blood on the floor from his beating. Nathan took a seat on the bench opposite him and sank down low; on the inside he was angry and fearful about the events that had unfolded. His best friend had tried to ruin everything, and Nathan could have been dying on the cathedral floor – and deserved it.

"You knew they were going to kill her, that they were going to kill them all. You fucking coward," Drake raged, his face painted with a hatred beyond words. He spat blood and stared at the ground, hunched over, unwilling to look Nathan in the eye. Nathan sighed; he could not find the words to respond; but he was eternally sorry and sick of pretending to be cold-hearted. Everything was his fault: leaving the red rose, killing the priest, bringing the Union in and letting the Great Houses burn. Maybe this was God's way of punishing him, a God he had forgotten about with such ease. Nathan pulled his friend up so he was sitting opposite him.

"You will pay for this, you coward; you will pay for everything."

"Shut up, Drake! I'm trying to think, give me a moment's peace."

Drake stopped. He couldn't understand Nathan's lack of understanding of the situation – his lack of feeling was madness. It didn't make any sense. Nathan had lost his mind and the worst part was that he didn't seem to care.

"Peace? A moment's peace? You wicked fool. You knew they were going to kill her, didn't you? Just say it!" Drake's rage broke the silence; he was so certain of the answer, but for his own sanity he had to hear it from Nathan himself.

"I knew something was going to happen and I tried

my best to warn her, but you wouldn't let me meet with her –"

"You would say anything, wouldn't you, to absolve yourself of blame. We were brothers, Nathan, and you have ruined everything."

"No! It is *you* who has ruined everything. Your drugs, drinking, gambling. I had it all planned out, I could have saved us all, we would be set in the Union, but *you* have ruined it."

"There are no words that can describe your actions, Nathan; there is nothing you can do to make things right. This world has tolerated you long enough. The people you have killed, men, women and children, the lives you have ruined – all whilst trying to justify it by claiming that you had no choice, that you were doing it for the greater good."

Drake destroyed him with these words, and although Nathan tried to maintain an intimidating sense of calm, he choked on a tear of sorrow. He had lost his voice as the world weighed him down. One awful decision, to trust the Union, had spiralled into a cascade of madness. He had been forced to dispose of any and all who posed his family any risk, that was all. Leave no stone unturned. Nathan looked at his friend and his lips trembled.

He battered the side of the van with heavy fists, over and over, taking out all the pain, all the anger on it, as Drake looked on speechless at his display of strength. Nathan took a moment to breathe, his head and his frame against the wall, his hands shaking.

"Evelyn is alive," he said.

Drake took a moment to process what he had said. He couldn't believe what he was hearing, but Nathan was serious. It was as if for a moment the pain lifted.

"W-what? How? I, I don't believe you, the blast killed them all."

"She is alive, and I'm sorry I couldn't tell you sooner."

"Where is she, is she okay?"

"She is safe."

"How – how is she alive?"

"Evelyn was the only one to survive the blast. She is in Sovereign Central Hospital, where they are taking Rose. Only you, Caleb and I know this; if the Council find out, they will kill us all. Do you understand?"

"I do." Drake nodded, and Nathan withdrew a key to unlock the handcuffs. Drake took a moment to feel his wrists and the red marks imprinted upon them.

"I do, but I need to see her." Drake's words were exactly what Nathan was afraid of.

"It isn't safe now, you have drawn their attention to you today, and they will want me to make an example of you."

Drake understood the severity of the situation. He would be a fool to believe that Nathan pulled all the strings. It was becoming apparent that the Council had full control of him.

"Did you mean to kill her, Nathan; did you mean to kill them all?" he asked.

"I only knew that something terrible was going to happen. I didn't know what, and when I did, it was too late. If the Council had told me, if they had given me any other choice, I would have done everything to stop it, but I had to secure my position and provide safety for Rose. I'm surprised the Council hasn't killed me already."

"What is it they want from you, what is it that is keeping you alive?"

"The Titan. All they want is the Titan, and I will give it to them."

"Well, what happens when they get the Titan?"

In truth, Nathan hadn't given that much thought. "They will ask me to sit upon the Council," he said, but as he said it aloud it pitched him into doubt. Drake's look of scepticism only made such thoughts worse.

"You don't seriously believe them, do you?"

"I do. Rogan has offered me a seat. I have his word. There is no going back. That's not to say I'm not worried – today you may have ruined everything." Nathan smirked, but his fear of the Council's retribution was very real. He didn't believe them – but they were the means to an end. His plan did not have a clear outcome; he would use the Titan to his advantage for as long as possible and after that hope for the best. The Council were said to be men of their word, but Rogan had betrayed the Ministry of Men already and further backstabbing was likely. Nathan knew too well the rumours of how the Council had disposed of their first leader, Elias Crane.

"When can I see her?" Drake asked, bringing Nathan's attention back. It dawned on Drake that every-thing had seemed surreal until now. He was still coming down from the glass, and as he pieced things together he cringed at what he had done; but the anger was still there.

"We will go to Sovereign Central. I'll make sure the Council thinks you are dead, but if they find out either you or Evelyn are alive, we're all finished. Do you understand?"

"I do," said Drake, and he stood up to hug his former friend.

After a moment, after so much pain, Nathan hugged him back and everything felt a little better. He knew Drake was unstable, and it hurt to see him like this. It had hurt to watch him pull the gun and face him like a monster. But now, for the first time in forever, everything seemed as if it was going to be okay. He knew that Rose would make it, the child too, and so would Evelyn. After the most difficult of times, Nathan and Drake stood across from one another, brothers once more.

14

INTELLIGENT DESIGN

The next day, Sam awoke wrapped in a grey blanket. The room was too bright as he lay on the bottom bunk; it creaked below him as he woke. Everything seemed like a dream, but it quickly dawned on him that he hadn't dreamt it at all. He had arisen from a deep sleep unlike any that had gone before, and it felt like someone was watching him. He turned around expecting to see Carter sitting at the kitchen counter, but he saw no one. The laboratory was silent except for the hum of its machines – he was alone. There was a deep hunger in his stomach; he was starving, aching. He looked for the suit, but it was nowhere to be found. He called out to Carter more than once, to no avail. There was, however, a satchel by his bedside, and he reached inside. All it contained was his notepad and pen. He flicked through the pages to see his drawings of the past few years.

Sam turned the pages to see manic drawings of a spaceship and a large floating device blocking out the sun. He flicked again and noticed something else. It was the girl – it was her – with her long flowing hair, and when he saw her, he knew it would all be worth it. He continued to flick through the pages to see other strange characters: a grey figure with spirals all over him, and even Doctor Carter, hunched over, clutching his chest. Sam also saw a little girl with plaits before he forced the notepad back into the satchel, feeling he had seen something he wasn't supposed to see. He didn't want to witness his madness; he wasn't ready for that.

Sam placed his legs out in front of him, creased his toes and put his feet firmly on the ground. Using the bunk bed, he struggled to his feet. He stayed still for a moment, afraid to take that first step, but then he did. He tumbled, caught his balance and walked forward to the counter and began rummaging for food. The cereal wasn't hard to find. Then he made for the fridge, poured from a carton of UHT milk and devoured all of it – he could eat the whole box if he wanted to, but there was no flavour.

As Sam wiped his mouth, the break-room doors slammed open; the shock cut through his easy mood, and as he looked out it registered that Carter was not there. Beyond the doors the laboratory was dark, and all of a sudden the sleeping quarters' lights went out too. Sam panicked; it felt as though he was being watched. He made for the light, but the switch did nothing; then the laboratory lit up, but the sleeping quarters were left in darkness. He did not want to be in the dark anymore and planned his move; he put faith in removing his hand from the safety of the kitchen surface and began to walk barefoot in nothing but his overalls through the break-room doors. As he walked through, they snapped shut behind him, not giving him a second.

They must be broken, he thought before the laboratory went black. Sam panicked, turned, and tried to prise it open.

"Carter! Enough of these games!" he shouted. There was a chill down his spine, and he felt the familiar panic of every morning, the fear and hopelessness of being alone in an unfamiliar place. And then he saw the figure, a green, child-like ghost, in the corner of his eye. Sam shouted and flinched, knocking things over as he scrambled backwards. Terrified, he tried to run but did not make it far and shuffled himself into the corner.

"Get away! Get away!" he shouted, barely able to open his eyes. When he did, there was nothing, only darkness – perhaps it had been another illusion. Yet as soon as he convinced himself he was imagining things, a green hand appeared to rest upon his shoulder and he turned to see a child staring back at him. Sam flinched again and it was gone, until he turned back, and there she stood, right in front of him, a small girl with plaits, wearing a summer dress, and smiling.

"Sam" she said, her voice soft and calm. "I didn't mean to scare you," she continued, a little shy and self-conscious, aware of the burden of being both human and machine.

"Who … what are you?"

"My name is Annie." She gave a curtsy as the room brightened slightly.

"You're a, you're a –"

"I'm a hologram." Annie nodded, before stepping forward, and then he saw the pixels. At first he had thought her a ghost, but the way her figure shimmered she seemed more a projection of light than a spectre. Sam was staring and Annie didn't seem too fond of his eyes on her – she was still a little girl after all.

"Hello, Annie," Sam replied. He waved his hand through her and she twitched slightly as Sam interrupted the projection. She stepped back, none too pleased.

"I'm sorry, this is a little strange, who are you? Where do you come from?" Sam was unsure whether he could comprehend what was in front of him, shaken as he was by the surprise of it all. Annie gave a small sigh, as if it would be illogical to explain herself.

"Artificial Neural Network Intelligence Experiment, that's what my name stands for – but that isn't who I am, and don't be sorry."

Her smile was a little unsettling, which was no surprise for she was unlike anything Sam had seen before. She looked about ten, twelve, or thereabouts; it was hard for Sam to know, as he had no experience with children. She looked at him in a strange way, as if greatly intrigued.

"I've been waiting for you. I thought you would never come, but here you are."

"What do you mean waiting for me?" asked Sam, her sprightly pace keeping her miles ahead of him. He scrambled upright, looking left and then right in fear that someone else might be listening, before peering closer and whispering.

"Can you get us out of here?"

Annie giggled before responding so faintly that it was hard to hear. "Oh Sam, the chances of escape are minimal, the bad man won't let you leave this place, not until you do what you came here to do."

It was becoming clear that this laboratory was not the place of dreams Carter had made it out to be – it was a prison indeed.

"The bad man? Carter?"

"No, Carter is the sad man. The bad man and his wicked, wicked witch."

"Who is the wicked witch?"

"Shh, they can hear you; I've said too much already." Annie placed a finger over her lips to hint at quietness and secrecy.

"Why am I here?"

"To turn on the Titan." Annie produced a 3D image of the massive ship lying dormant above them. It spun around slowly, and Sam realised he had seen such a blueprint before, as a memory of his parents' work returned.

"Can't you turn it on?" he asked. A fair question, but one that Annie took offence to: she folded her arms and looked displeased, for turning the Titan on was the one thing she wouldn't do.

"You look just like Jonathan, Sam," she said before shaking her head and skipping around the room. His father's name clicked in his head like the cocking of a gun. She disappeared before he could reach out a hand and ask her to wait. The lights brightened and Sam summoned the courage to pick himself up. He brushed the dust off his overalls, alone once more in a room full of blueprints, drawings and designs for great machines. He contemplated her few words as he looked at the syringes on the side, the microscope and piles of documents. He looked up to see the many cameras pointing every which way; it made him wonder who was watching. Annie's words had only provoked more questions, as had Carter's. He turned his attention to the giant metal cube and placed a hand upon it. It was so cold. He looked at the hatch, almost at shoulder height. Before he could give it a proper inspection the lights dimmed again and Annie was right behind him.

"Don't touch that," she said as he jumped back in surprise. He was still on edge, unable to get used to the way she sneaked up on him.

"Shit!"

"Don't swear, I don't like swearing."

"Why would I care what you like?" he said, still in a state of bewilderment.

"Because I know you, Sam, I know you're a good person who shouldn't swear."

"How would you know anything about me? You're a machine."

"You've hurt my feelings."

"You don't have feelings, you're a machine."

Her eyes began to water, and he immediately regretted what he'd said. Annie moved back from him with a frown and Sam wasn't sure what to do.

"I'm sorry, I – this whole thing is just so strange."

"I understand; there hasn't been a Royle on this earth who isn't strange."

"You knew my parents?" he asked, and Annie could see how he felt by his eyes, though she would make no attempt to hold back what he needed to hear.

"They *made* me, Sam."

That statement made him rather uncomfortable: this *hologram* thought his parents had made her. It was a strange thing to imagine.

"That makes you my –"

"No – no, it doesn't," Sam insisted, knowing that she meant to use the word "sister". He leant against the cold metal box and sighed. "They were always too caught up with work to care, and that's what got them killed."

Sam held them responsible for their own deaths, he always had. Behind his words was an expression of pain and anxiety at the very mention of them, and it didn't take long for Annie to assess this.

"They didn't want to send you away, they loved you very much. Most of their time was spent thinking about you while they tried to escape after being forced to give you up when they were taken."

"They mean nothing to me," he said with sadness in his heart, faking every word. Annie could sense when he was telling the truth and when he wasn't, but didn't want to upset him – no, it was too soon for that.

"You don't mean that – they loved you," she said, moving closer.

"I-I don't even know what happened to them." He sighed.

"For a long time their work helped the world, but Infinity Research was taken over. They couldn't leave, were forced to work after the war; a friend tried to help them but couldn't."

"What about Carter?" asked Sam, remembering that he was nowhere to be found. The worst came to mind.

"What about him?"

"I don't trust him," he said blankly.

"The Doctor has his problems; he's been a prisoner here for over twenty years. I can't see beyond this room, but I sense fear in him when he's around."

Sam understood why Carter was afraid: twenty years in this place, in this shining, wretched place.

"How do I do what I came here to do?"

"You can't – only I can turn on the Titan," said Annie, shaking her head.

"Start the Titan, then I can leave. My parents would have wanted that."

"The Titan will never fly, I made a promise," said Annie with such conviction that Sam's heart sank; he could guess who that promise had been made to.

"I didn't choose to be here, you have to get me out of here," he demanded.

"Unfortunately, I can't."

"This is hopeless," said Sam in frustration. He sat on the floor, leaning against a large cabinet, and pushed his hand through his hair.

"Don't be sad, Sam," she replied.

"Don't be sad? My life was taken from me; I was left

to rot after losing everything. I can't even remember anything. Now I'm here waiting to die."

Annie could sense his feelings; she had a heightened understanding that no other machine or human being was capable of – a burden and a strength.

"I can give you something that no one else can," she said with a reassuring smile.

"What would that be?"

"What if I said I could tell you everything about the life you have forgotten, help you remember."

"How would you do that?"

"Are you ready?"

Sam pondered but didn't have an answer. Did he really want to know, or did he want it all to be over before it had begun? The idea of his past made him feel a sense of looming traumatic stress.

"I will never be ready, but the least I can do is try."

Annie looked at him with hopeful eyes before giving an affirming nod and darting into his brain. Everything was white, then black, and then there was a green flash before he was weightless inside his own mind. A vision of glowing colour, a fourth dimension, and heightened euphoria overwhelmed him. There was no time, only space. On the outside, his eyes rolled back in his head and his body slumped against the workbench, but he could see more clearly than ever before. A world of code and consciousness consumed him as images of his past filled his mind's eye. For a moment he could not breathe, and when he tried to catch his breath he crashed into a pool of water, a pond.

When Sam pulled his head above the water, he saw

in the distance his childhood self sitting in a playground. When teachers came for him, the child ran to the pond in the rain, to rest upon a fallen tree and hide. The adults marched forward, searching with spotlights. Sam knew his childhood self was hiding in the rain from the news of his parents' death. The teachers searched far and wide, but it was a girl who found him and comforted him, a button-nosed little girl with hazel eyes and a ponytail, who dried his tears before the strangers took him away. Hope held his hand, hugged him close and said to be brave, so he was.

She is real, Sam thought; and then he remembered the other school, darker and greyer, a Kingdom flag on its high walls. It was the military academy where he would learn what it meant to push, to bleed, to climb a rope, command a unit, master science, engineering, and dream of her. Hope would visit when she could, and though she had grown into a woman her hazel eyes always stayed the same. They would laugh, they would cry, and they would feel their togetherness even when far apart. His heart sank at those memories; there was no way he could be prepared for all this information and it overwhelmed him.

Annie revealed each door, and as she did, she unlocked another part of him, no matter how alien it was. Thousands of bits of data flew, building a picture of continuity. In the Academy, he saw fellow orphans, his brothers, those lost in service. Everything flashed before his eyes: classrooms, bunk beds, the odd smell of too many boys, the taste of military meals – it all came flooding back to him, and to her. Hope was with him through it all. He felt such fear and hate, but then also motivation, determination, and underneath it all love for the girl who remained such a mystery. He could see her now, almost hold her, feel her warmth … and then it all came back.

At eighteen, one door called more than any other. New Year at the Old Abbey Gardens. A thousand bright lights flickering on fairground rides, with the sounds of laughter and screaming. It was the perfect night, though they had little but each other. He remembered running into the guards, seeing the building flicker into derelict blackness, and the lights going out, but they came back when he felt her hand again, like he had felt her hand all those years earlier, next to the pond in the schoolyard. It always brought him back.

"Stay for the fireworks," she said, and so he did. They lit up the sky, a myriad different colours, a beautiful display expanding the universe. It was beyond anything he could have ever imagined. Being with her was infinite for a moment, and he tried to tell himself to stay here, to run away, to never return to the military, to leave it all behind. He saw his younger self ask Hope to marry him, and how gently she said no. She said to ask again when he returned. She was so beautiful against the backdrop of fireworks, there was never a doubt in her lit-up eyes of his return, and Sam savoured the moment, even though he didn't know that it was the last time he would ever see her.

It was the most beautiful time in his life, and given that most of his life lacked such beauty it shone brighter than a million other beautiful things ever could. So Sam rewound the moment so she could ask again.

"Will you at least stay for the fireworks?"

"I wouldn't miss them for the world."

He drifted away from that moment; it was the grandest memory he could ever ask for. There was nothing more he wanted, but it would be dangerous to stay in such a world of dreams. Annie pushed him on to see the fighting, his strength and agility. The battlefield, fallen friends, and the shaking behind bullet-ridden walls, ready to pop up and move forward as those around him trembled. A sergeant pushing forward offered his hand and Sam took hold. They pushed together against blinding explosions and the deafening blast of gunfire. It was all for her, it was all for them. There were medals, funerals, horns, and shots fired into the air for those lost. Salutes, handshakes, dinners and dances – but past it all he saw Hope, for she was still waiting for him.

Then the darkness came, memories looming in the shadows. Dreams of his parents' murders produced sketches, strange visions of figures from the future, odd delusions that didn't make sense. Visions of great ships, of children, of a flying sun. He kept such things bottled up, as no one would ever understand until he found those who killed his parents. The Ministry of Men – they were real. He searched, interrogated, worked alone, and when he was close to finding an answer, they took him in the night and broke him.

Everything stopped as he stared into a mirror, drooling, with a drip in his arm, dosed up in the

Asylum, all alone, wasting away. He remembered the confusion, the pain, the lack of coordination, the memory problems and, most of all, the piercing headaches. Sam didn't know what to say or how to react to himself in such a state. All he could do was watch with a silent and desperate hate. He locked eyes with himself and begged to push on, to get out, escape, but it was too late. Then he felt as if he had screamed at himself like this before but thought it might be just another hint of madness. The mass of information was overwhelming.

"Stop!" he shouted, covering his ears and closing his eyes, wishing the world away. Slowly he was sucked through darkness and back into his body; he caught his breath before sitting up in shock. He tried to breathe, tried to feel, tried to look around and use his eyes, but it took time to realise his surroundings were there.

"I'm sorry; I know it hurts but you had to see the truth through the illusion. You are much greater than you think. If I could place a hand on your shoulder to comfort you, I would – but I can't," said Annie with regret, holding his hand until the feelings had slowly passed through him.

"I've seen it all, but it isn't the same as remembering."

"No, but with time you will remember."

"Well, what now? Now I know who I am, how does that make a difference in here, how will any of this help me?"

"That's a question I don't have an answer to, but we will find a way together, I promise. There is much more

I have to show you, although you still aren't ready for some of it."

Annie reassured him with a kind smile, but Sam had seen what he once was, and it unsettled him. He wasn't strong, or a soldier, he wasn't bedridden and ill. He just was, and he didn't have to be anything else. Understanding himself would take time, patience and determination. If there was only one thing left for him to do on this earth now, it was that. He pulled himself to his feet and struggled along the workbench to a notepad and a pen and began to draw.

15

THE FLOOD

Lanterns lit the way through winding cobbled passages. Having abandoned the map, Lydia ran through the maze following Markus's lead. The tunnels gave her an eerie feeling after the terror of yesterday's run, squeezing through crevices and struggling against iron bars to the squeal of rats and the shudders of her suit. Today she was light on her feet, but with only a few hours' rest she could think only of her parents and revenge. The map she was tasked to memorise was pointless, giving a thousand different routes. Behind her, Youssef's footsteps echoed heavily, the giant thuds making it hard to concentrate. Just up ahead she watched Markus and Gabriel stride along in competition with each other, seeming as if they could run forever if the other challenged them to. It was easy to be nervous around them; it was easy to question why she had agreed to such a thing – but she needed a good fight.

"How long do these tunnels go on for?" Lydia asked.

"Forever, if you go the wrong way!" Markus shouted back. His voice echoed around the chamber. Another turn, and another, down low and then back up again. After miles of running, turning left and right, then scaling a rickety ladder, there was moonlight coming from one of the tunnels. Each led out to a larger opening in the sewer system. At the end of the moonlit tunnel was freedom, far from the confines of Sovereign. The smell and beauty of grass, the moon and stars that most would yearn for, didn't lighten Lydia's mood. A cold feeling remained at her core: part of her had died yesterday. She readied herself for revenge in whatever form it would take. If every life brought a little bit of herself back, then some day she might smile again.

Ahead, an old rusted van awaited them. They travelled for ten minutes down the valley as Youssef weighed down the front left-hand side of the vehicle. Lydia was opposite Gabriel and watched him chew gum and caress his rifle case incessantly, so she took to looking out of the window. It was a quiet, moonlit night, calm, but not as dark as they had hoped. Behind them Lydia could see the outskirts of the city in the distance; somehow it seemed much larger from here. Amongst it all somewhere was the flat she had abandoned and, far away on the other side, those she had not had time to say goodbye to.

"You're facing the wrong way," said Gabriel, preparing his rifle; he screwed on the silencer, adjusted the reticule and observed Nexa, the watchtowers, the tents and trucks. "There they are; there's enough food and ammunition here to last us a year," he said, noting the two trucks within the compound that their scouts had been watching since the Union's arrival. They were filled with supplies, mostly food to be given out during the current crisis. They didn't appear to have been unloaded yet and Markus's plan seemed one of promise after all.

"How many enemies do you see?" asked Markus as Gabriel scanned the area.

"Ten, give or take. Two watchtowers – two guards in one, three in the other. But many more below, I suspect, most likely within the tents. Now's the time, if at all."

Markus nodded and gave his signal; he ran with Youssef and Lydia toward the compound in the darkness. Lydia powered ahead in her suit and looked up at the tower looming above her. A guard turned the watchtower's corner and spotted her right away; caught by surprise, he opened his mouth to shout for help when one of Gabriel's bullets went straight through his forehead. He fell to the floor, limp and lifeless. The other two guards attempted to pick up their rifles but fell swiftly after Gabriel's second and third shots.

Youssef and Markus reached the fence and Markus pulled out a pair of pliers and began clipping as Youssef kept guard next to him. The chatter in the second tower was also silenced by Gabriel's shots. The fence was tough and even Markus's robotic hand struggled to rip through the thick wire. Out of the corner of Youssef's eyes he saw something flash past him. Lydia jumped through the air, landing on one of the towers. She swung down to a guard on watch and broke his neck before making for the fence. By the time Markus cut through the fourth link, Lydia was opposite him on the other side, and with one mighty pull they ripped the fence open. Markus looked down at the pliers and placed them back in his back pocket. In silence they began to move through the compound in the shadows, past tents where soldiers were playing music, laughing and drinking. There were many voices, but they soon made it to the trucks.

"Can you hot-wire one of these?" Markus whispered. Lydia replied with a simple nod. They took a truck each, Youssef climbed into the back of Markus's, and took his 50-cal machine gun off his shoulder. He set it up, rather proud of turning a simple supply truck into a deadly weapon.

Markus hot-wired the first truck and sparked the ignition; moments later Lydia's truck followed. A spotlight shone down from the second watchtower: they had missed a sleeping guard who must now have noticed the bodies. Sirens bellowed as arc lights came on all around, with the shouts of soldiers readying themselves. They poured from the tents as Youssef's machine gun hammered hell upon them, bullets ripping through flesh and fabric alike. The soldiers scattered, diving to the floor or running for cover, taken by surprise, unarmed and unready. Lydia put her foot down and tried to pick up as much speed as possible; the trucks were slow to accelerate but did the job well enough. Her truck roared towards the front gate but didn't pick up enough speed. The gates crumpled on impact but became wrapped around her truck. A heavy chain had stopped them from breaking. Youssef continued to hold the soldiers off. The crackle and smoke of gunfire erupted all around, and in her panic Lydia didn't know what to do. She hammered the acceleration, revving repeatedly; the fence buckled but didn't break, only wrapping itself further around the truck like cling film. The soldiers started shooting back. Youssef's kill count was growing, but there were far more men than the band had anticipated, and with every passing second more and more returned fire.

Upon the rocky hillside, high above the compound, Gabriel was taking shot after shot, dropping more than enough to keep them at bay. He knew something was wrong, though, and he stopped firing and changed his target. Lining up the shot, he held his breath before shooting the chain, breaking it to pieces. The bullet ricocheted through Lydia's passenger window, right into the passenger headrest, meeting the metal behind. For a moment she stared through the hole in the windscreen, unable to believe how close that was. She turned to her right and had the feeling that her father was watching, before bringing herself back to what was going on around her. The truck pushed through and Markus followed. They roared up the hill towards Gabriel. He opened the door and climbed up the steps with his rifle, cool and calm.

"Nice shooting," she said.

"Always; but if you want to see something really great, watch this ..." He gave a cheeky smile and took something from his pocket, a remote detonator. The remaining soldiers had got in their vehicles and were ready to give chase when he clicked the button. The watchtowers collapsed, crushing the broken fence with debris, thus delaying the soldiers' chase. Powering down the road, the band created some distance from them; victory was in the air, but the killing hadn't itched Lydia's scratch. She still felt numb, so cold and heartless. Empty. And though she knew Markus would be happy, as he could feed his people for the foreseeable future, even that didn't make the moment any sweeter.

After driving back to the large sewer exit, they turned off the headlights. Markus's truck pulled to a halt and Lydia did the same, then they got out to regroup. Youssef climbed out of the back, laughing in triumph as he did.

"Did you see!" he shouted. Markus shared a smile with him but was worried, knowing the task was not over, as Gabriel polished his rifle in eager anticipation of their next move. Before anyone replied, the ground began to shake and that stopped them in their tracks. The sound of unfamiliar laughter came from Lydia's truck as an unknown soldier revealed himself. A man in United Front uniform climbed down and threw a radio to the ground in front of them. Markus ran up to him, knocking him down with a mighty swing, and stood over him gripping his collar.

"What did you do!" he shouted, shaking him back and forth as the officer spat blood from his mouth.

"Markus Vance, I knew it was you." His voice was slurred, as if he had been drinking. "Back-up is on the way – who knew I'd be getting drunk in the back of this truck when you turned up! I'll get a medal for this!"

Markus hit him again and again and the man lost consciousness. "Control yourself, brother," Gabriel shouted, pulling him away, but Markus was lost in panic. For the first time, Lydia saw fear in his eyes as the sound of armoured vehicles rumbled in the near distance and fog lights lit the horizon.

"What do we do?" asked Youssef. Lydia saw that Markus had frozen along with his brother.

"Gabriel, do you have any more of that C4 to blow this entrance shut?" she asked.

"We're all out. We have guns, thousands of rounds, but nothing that can take down this entrance safely," he replied. They looked at Markus, but for the first time he was unsure of what to do. Their enemies were closing in around them and his people needed him now more than ever, but his mind was stuck. It was only a matter of time before the Union soldiers found a way through and took everything, shooting everyone in their path.

Lydia spoke. "Take the trucks as far as they can go, then head back to warn the others. Get as many able men to fight as you can."

Markus looked down the hillside at their enemies coming from afar. "You don't have to do this. These are my people," he said.

"I don't have people. I don't have anything anymore, anything to live for, at least let me go out doing something good," Lydia said.

Markus didn't have time to talk her down, or say

thank you, or anything; he just nodded. "What are you waiting for? Go!"

"I'm not going anywhere, I'm our best shot. You need me," said Gabriel.

Markus didn't want to risk his brother, but he was right. They shared a look, more than words could say, knowing what had to be done to defend those inside.

Youssef took the 50-cal from his shoulder and tossed it to Lydia, and her suit swayed to absorb the impact. "You will need it," he said.

Markus and Youssef got in the trucks. They started driving down the widest tunnel, the only way back to the grave smugglers in a vehicle. Lydia set up the machine gun on its bipod as a convoy of Union trucks gathered upon the hillside. At least they had the high ground.

Readying his rifle, Gabriel took off the silencer as a form of intimidation; armour-piercing rounds should penetrate the reinforced glass of the enemy vehicles, he thought. For his first shot he went for the windscreen, but the bullet bounced off. His second cracked the glass. His third went right through and into the driver's chest. The first armoured vehicle wobbled out of control and spun, crashing into another. But it was a small victory for there were five more trucks intact thundering towards them.

Lydia hadn't fired a shot yet but now was the time; she put a finger on the trigger and was about to pull.

"Wait," said Gabriel.

"Why?"

"I only fired to make them charge," he said; so,

Lydia waited. Gabriel knew something she didn't: the reason they used this entrance for supply runs. If they were ever chased, the valley became its own defence; it opened wide, then dipped down and back up again towards the entrance. The trucks thundered down the slope at speed and were confronted with blackness. Within the darkness, they moved too fast for the condition of ground in front of them. It dipped sharply into a deep ditch before a steep grassy rise. It was an immovable natural wall, hidden by the dip; the grass had grown over it as if it wasn't there. The trucks smashed into it at pace, bringing them to an abrupt halt. They were too well armoured to crumple, but anyone not expecting the impact or not wearing a seatbelt was going to be a mess. Multiple soldiers vacated the trucks while others squirmed on the floor, moaning. There were forty men and all of them were shaken by the impact.

Gabriel made light work of firing round after round. The Union soldiers returned fire, but he felt invincible at this range. Lydia let loose on the 50-cal's trigger, thundering bullets down upon the soldiers below, striking fear into their hearts. Gabriel continued to take shot after shot, wiping them out. If he saw an elbow or an ankle, he took it from them. If he saw a head or a shoulder, he took it from them. His confidence grew with his kill count as smoke billowed in the air and the familiar smell of gun smoke filled his nostrils. Gabriel was born for this, no matter how much he regretted it.

Lydia flew through her bullets. They were fortunate

that the soldiers were stuck out in the open. Under-cover, Gabriel and Lydia looked at each other and shared a smile as they started to believe that against all odds they might just survive.

In the darkness, a shadow stood waiting on the hill-side, smoking a cigarette, too far away to be seen clearly. He flicked his cigarette to the ground and steadied his rifle with a mean look and grit in his eye. It was Caleb Walker, Nathan's right-hand man. He lay down and took aim.

"Idiots," he muttered to himself, staring at the soldiers below. Adjusting his aim, he saw Lydia. "Well, I don't believe my fucking eyes, what a pretty little thing we have here. Now, where's this sniper?" Adjusting his scope, he fired a thunderous shot. Lydia flinched and stopped firing; she turned to see Gabriel looking down at a wide round bloody hole in his chest. He fell to his knees as if in prayer, holding his chest as blood began to pour.

Caleb turned his aim on Lydia, but she had already scrambled towards Gabriel behind cover, and was holding him as he lay. "No, no, no, no, no," she pleaded as the gunfire stopped for a moment.

Gabriel coughed, growing pale and lifeless. Shaking his head, he couldn't seem to make eye contact with her. "You have to go … Make them follow the middle tunnel." He grabbed her arm and pulled her close. "*Swim*," he whispered.

Caleb looked on through his scope; he couldn't get a clean shot, but *how sweet*, he thought. Piercing the night skies with a wolf whistle, he lifted his left arm as more trucks flew past him. Jumping on the back of one, he advanced with them. At pace a small army of engines thundered down the hill and this time they went around the valley to avoid the large dip the rest had fallen into. Caleb lit a cigarette as he flew through the evening breeze on the open back of his truck.

There was no time; Lydia had to move. She stroked Gabriel's cheek and whispered farewell. He had said the middle tunnel, but there were too many to choose from, seven or eight. The feelings of yesterday flooded back as she dived into one at random. She waited in the dark, listening to the rumbling engines approaching. All she could think about was her parents and how they must have felt the same yesterday.

Markus, where are you? she thought, pinned against the tunnel wall and poking her head around the corner. The shadows of soldiers came with echoes of stomping boots, sealing off any chance of escape. A crowd of soldiers had gathered at the entrance, but there were many pathways for them to choose, so if Lydia was quiet she would stay hidden for a few minutes.

"Little girl, come out here! It's time to join your father!" Caleb shouted, his voice echoing through the tunnels.

"You cowards!" she shouted back. His attempt to bait her had worked but they could not tell from which tunnel her voice came.

"Show yourself and I might even let your friend live," said Caleb, trying to work out which tunnel she was in.

Lydia could see him at the front of the crowd,

wearing a similar exo-suit to her, with a sick smile on his face; he loved moments like these. Lining up a shot with her rifle, she dared to pull the trigger and a soldier behind Caleb let out a yelp before falling to the floor. Caleb began to chuckle; he looked up and pointed to her tunnel. "That one!" he shouted, and the soldiers flooded in.

Shit, she thought. Turning to run, the exo-suit gave her an advantage, but bursts of gunfire followed her, ricocheting off the walls. She kept pace ahead of them and disappeared into the distance, but the stomping of boots filled the tunnel, growing ever closer.

The soldiers ran and ran until they reached a large opening and piled into a vast chamber. Raising their guns, they looked around the huge empty concrete room as a sea of searchlights cut through the darkness. Pipework, scaffolding and large turbines filled the place. Then they saw a very large shadow on the roof.

"Come down now, we're tired of your games," shouted Caleb, but Lydia didn't respond. Instead, there was a loud creaking of metal turning without oil. It looked as if the shadow was turning something. A drip of water landed on Caleb's forehead and he wiped it from his brow as a rumbling sound came from afar. Lydia reached towards the chest piece of her exo-suit and pulled off a mouth guard attached to a tube. Caleb spotted her up above and was about to take a shot when a thundering rush of water came blasting into the storm drain to swallow his men. Caleb pulled his mouth guard off his exo-suit and placed it over his mouth just before the water slammed against him.

~

Markus and Youssef drove at speed through the tunnel as it narrowed around them. The roofs of the trucks scraped on loose bricks, knocking them down into the tunnel. It was only two miles, but the trucks were slow while Markus's mind raced. The Union soldiers had found an entrance and soon more would come, and then it would be too late for everyone. Men, women and children would be executed or shipped off to camps. He didn't want to accept it, but he had a looming feeling that this was the end of the grave smugglers.

The tunnel grew cramped and the trucks came to a grinding halt at the entrance to his hideout. Markus banged on the wooden door over and over again with his mighty fist. A peephole opened, and eyes peered out before signalling others to open the door.

"Markus!" shouted a stout young man, slow to see the awareness of danger in his leader's eyes. "Is something wrong?"

"Dylan, my son, raise the alarm."

Dylan's expression changed from one of acceptance to one of fear; he was not ready for the task bestowed upon him. He ran towards the squat tower that housed the alarm. Markus's people gathered in the main square. Markus was afraid but he dared not show it; there were enemies at his gates and far too many of his people were unable to take up arms. All the men, women and children gathered together, waiting for him to speak, but

Markus didn't seem ready, he was nervous and anxious all at once.

"The enemy are at the south tunnel; take everything you can and leave. I need able soldier on me, and those with basic training to lead the escape."

"Escape?" asked Dylan.

"Union soldiers are at our doors; we must flee to the North."

There was silence until every able-bodied man and woman stood up and moved towards him. Atilla's mother, Rhea, had another young child with her; she seemed angry and afraid. "Don't do this, why are you going back? We can all go together. There is no need to break us apart," she pleaded.

"Gabriel is there, I won't let him die for me," Markus said, holding back how he really felt for her. "You must go and alert the other communes; Dylan, you will lead the others."

"And where will we go?" asked Dylan, now ready to earn his stripes.

"Take the supply trucks up the Northern Pass, get as far from the city as you can after warning our other brothers."

"Yes, sir," he replied without hesitation; though he knew the North held no promise, he wouldn't voice his opinion aloud out of respect. Dylan's family was in Sovereign and he would have to accept the thought of never seeing them again.

The grave smugglers were loyal and willing to do anything their leader asked; they said their goodbyes as instructed. Fathers left their sons and mothers left their children; parents tried to be brave as the crowd divided. Markus ran as fast as he could, and Youssef tried to keep up. They took to their vehicles, dirt bikes and jeeps, before taking off with a small force behind them. Down the tunnels they went, Markus roaring with speed on his bike. He turned to the truck to see Atilla hanging off the back; he was a straggler they didn't need, so he dropped behind to see what the boy was doing.

"Atilla, what do you think you're doing here? Go back to your mother, she needs your protection," he shouted.

"I want to fight with you," the little boy replied.

"I don't have time for this, stay at the back."

Though it had only been a matter of minutes, Markus was terrified for Lydia and Gabriel. He thought of how bad things could get if they were captured, or worse. Unable to bear the guilt on his conscience, he flew back down the cobbled tunnel ahead of the rest. Awkward twists and turns and bumps in the road jerked him, but he was going too fast to care.

He played the moment in his head over and over: roaring into battle whilst riding through the ranks, spraying bullets from his assault rifle while leaning over the handlebars, certain of glory in death … But when it came to it, there was light at the end and no gunfire. His hopes of Lydia and Gabriel holding the enemy off dwindled and a waiting wall of guns took his imagination.

Markus charged valiantly from the end of the tunnel, mid-skid. The assault rifle was positioned on the handlebars, in his good hand. Powering through, he expected a warrior's end, but found mostly soaking wet Union bodies. A few stray guns began to fire, bouncing off his dirt bike as Markus hesitated, but in an instant the machine guns behind him rained bullets down upon the remaining soldiers. Youssef screamed whilst shooting from the top of one of the trucks; another threw a grenade into the crowd as Markus and the others went to work with a swift barrage of gunfire, roaring and pushing forward at the few who remained.

Screams, curses and wailing from the pain of their wounds resounded through the chamber as Markus spied a familiar face in the distance. Caleb Walker, Nathan Sahl's second in command, was hunched at the hillside entrance. He was barely standing, and their eyes met only for a moment. Caleb was drenched, bruised and broken. Completely caught off guard, his stare alone said more than words could. The chaos of hot lead was ending lives on both sides; Markus watched as friends and family fell around him. The trucks were full of bullet holes, but Markus's men pushed on regardless. Caleb must have known his men were done for: he retreated, scrambling backwards. It was chaos as he darted from the tunnel, running as fast as the exo-suit could carry him to the nearest vehicle. He started the engine bitterly; it wasn't like him to run, not at all, but he had never been faced with defeat before, and Markus could see the cowardice in Caleb's eyes as he left.

The dust settled around them and the moans and groans of the injured swiftly took over from gunfire. Markus felt great pride: they had won an important battle and bought his people time to escape. He looked around and saw the grey and red Union uniforms – redder than ever before. He pushed on to the outside of the tunnel where Caleb's vehicle was disappearing into the distance. He looked around desperately for Lydia and Gabriel, careful not to step on any of the bodies around him. Neither of them was anywhere to be found. He heard echoing footsteps behind him and he turned to see a shadow stumbling from the drain tunnel, shaking, moving dizzily, almost drunkenly toward him. Markus knew from the skeletal outline of the suit that it was Lydia.

He walked towards her and knew straightaway that something was wrong. He took a few more steps and noticed she was shaking. Even with the suit's support, moving was a struggle; she came forward, off balance, dragging her feet, and as they met she fell into his arms.

"Where is Gabriel?" he asked.

"He … he's gone," she said, gasping, almost passing out from exhaustion. Markus held back the scream he felt inside, and the tears; it was as if a part of him was gone. He could not find the words to fathom the loss. For the first time, he felt completely alone. He carried Lydia over to a drier part of the tunnel entrance and laid her down, placing a jacket under her head.

"I'm sorry," she whispered softly before closing her eyes once more. Markus looked around; of the twenty men who had accompanied him, only four remained, eight including himself, Lydia, Youssef and Atilla. The water around them ran red against his boots.

My brother, my brother. Markus took the rifle off his shoulder and with both hands battered it against the wet ground. His metal fist bashed the stock to pieces, then he dropped it to the floor, remaining on his knees in the water running red.

"Markus, what shall we do?" asked Atilla in his boyish voice. Youssef stepped in front of the boy and placed a huge arm between them.

"Give him time, little one," said Youssef in a deep, broken voice. Markus stormed a long way out of the sewer entrance and into the field; there was no sign of Gabriel's body anywhere. He climbed onto a large rock and looked down upon the valley where the seven abandoned trucks lay riddled with bullet holes from Gabriel's favourite weapon. This loss cut deeper than any other: his only family member, someone who had been there from the start, was gone. All he had left was his people, and they would be scattered and running for their lives by now.

"I can't lead them without you, brother, I can't," he said to himself in mourning.

Markus sat upon the rock for half an hour in silence to grieve. He heard Youssef's footsteps approaching and he was not alone. Lydia had followed him; she had a slight limp but otherwise seemed okay. Markus didn't turn to face them; he was not in the mood, but they would not leave him.

"Did you flood the storm drain?" he asked in a quiet voice, desperate not to mention his brother, for the thought alone would kill him.

"I turned the wheel and opened the flood gate. I'm sorry," Lydia replied, teary-eyed. "I didn't see them take him."

"They took his body." Markus made a fist, clenching it tight. He could not believe it; anger, denial and sickness took over. The right to bury his brother had been denied him.

"They did, but we can make them pay."

"Caleb Walker and Nathan Sahl will die for this." There was less anger and more conviction in his voice now. Lydia understood his feelings all too well and knew what had to be done, but the thought of revenge wasn't bringing any satisfaction after drowning endless enemies.

"Let's gather your soldiers," she said.

"They need to re-join the others; I'm not fit to lead them." Markus shook his head; he could see Atilla and the others staring at him from afar. They had never seen him so down before, and he felt weak and ashamed.

"Markus! I hope you are okay," said Atilla with tears in his eyes as he ran towards them.

"I will be fine," Markus lied.

"Only one of the trucks works and we won't be able to start the Union ones – what do we do?" asked Faro, interrupting them. He was one of Markus's trusted men, more a smuggler than a soldier.

"Take the truck, re-join our people near the city and go north."

"Yes, Markus," said Faro, losing no time.

"Atilla, you must protect your mother."

"We will protect her together," said the boy.

Markus placed a hand upon Atilla's shoulder and with it came the weight of separation. "I can't go with you, I am not fit to lead," he admitted with remorse.

Markus could see the heartbreak in the boy's eyes, the disbelief and denial. He then looked around at the more mature faces in his party, who silently respected his decision. They would not ask him to stay. Many had lost as much as he had, many knew the same pain, and many were eager to ensure that their loved ones did not meet the same fate. Markus, however, needed time to grieve. But Atilla was a child and had already lost his father; now the man he turned to for the same guidance was leaving him behind.

"You can't leave!" he shouted, folding his arms and backing away from Markus.

"I can't come with you, I'm sorry."

Atilla kicked him and threw small punches until his pain turned to tears and Markus hugged him tight.

"Faro, Henry, Liam and Zoe, regroup with the others, take the trucks and get him to his mother."

Faro nodded and picked Atilla up from behind, throwing him over his shoulder. Atilla kicked and screamed endlessly, begging him to let go.

"You coward!" cried the boy as they dragged him away to the truck. Markus tried his best not to look but the sound haunted him; it broke his heart, but it was too dangerous for any of them to be around him – they would be safer on their own. Atilla banged on the windows at Markus as tears rolled down his cheeks. Markus placed a hand on his heart, hiding the tear that left his eye. He waited and waited, unable to move until the sound of something scurrying in the sewer took his attention. Youssef looked at him, bemused, while Lydia was too busy shivering to notice. Markus ran back to find a young red-headed Union Front soldier crawling towards a pistol just out of his reach. Markus pulled him back and rolled him over, then punched him with his heavy metal fist. The soldier shrieked.

"Where is Caleb Walker!" he shouted, pulling him close and then slamming him down.

"I don't know," the soldier pleaded as Lydia stumbled in to intervene.

"Stop this!" she shouted, but Markus pushed her back with ease before going at him again.

Youssef came forward and grabbed Markus by his jacket. "Enough!" He threw him backwards. "You will become one of them!"

Markus stared up at the giant. He watched Youssef pick up the soldier by his leg and pat him down. He sat the soldier upright and noticed how young he was.

"Run along now. If I see you turn back, I will break your little arms and legs, then I will tie them in a knot, understand?"

"Y-y-yes, sir." The young Union soldier nodded before turning to sprint away.

When Markus saw his age, he realised that he was not okay. He turned and walked back out of the tunnel and made his way to the boulder he had sat upon earlier. He remembered the old ways of the Cannon Islands, where Gabriel and he were born. Neither of their parents hailed from the island, but it was a smugglers' port and the brothers had spent their early years growing up there before moving on. The island marked the graves of their dead with rocks, he remembered, and he now began to collect rocks from the ground. One by one he moved them whilst thinking about Gabriel and their childhood. He imagined his little brother alongside him, helping him shift the rocks as they had done for their mother. Hours later, he admired his work from the boulder, where Gabriel's spirit sat alongside him.

16

SUNLIGHT

S am had sat for hours in the laboratory; his body was weak, but his mind was much stronger. It had taken time for his existential shock to fade and for him to process everything. Annie had shown him so much already; she seemed to be the only person, or thing, who could understand him right now, and Sam had confided in her, for she knew more about him than he knew himself. Though she was only a sophisticated piece of programming, there was something very real about her. It had been quite some time since Carter had gone and Sam had barely noticed, being too busy learning about himself. He was drawing sketches again, of fires, flaming figures and the curious cube in the corner.

The sound of the large heavy doors opening interrupted his train of thought, and then he heard Carter's slow limping footsteps trail across the floor. He carried a tension with him, as if he had received some rather bad news. Distressed and nervous, he walked into the living quarters and went to the kitchen counter. He flicked on the hot tap and it started to steam, a loud bubbling leading to a prolonged rumble.

"Tea or coffee?" he shouted through the doorway whilst grabbing two mugs from the cupboard above.

I liked one and hated the other, Sam thought to himself, but he could not remember which was which. "Coffee," he guessed, before going on to say, "You didn't introduce me to Annie."

"Ah, no. I thought it was best that she introduced herself."

Sam couldn't see through the doorway that Carter's hands were shaking; everything Monroe had said filled his mind, but he had to push on, for his family.

"Argh!' Carter shouted, having scalded the skin on his hand, and dropped the mug. Sam and Annie turned towards him as it crashed into the sink below.

"Are you okay?" Sam asked, but it was obvious he wasn't.

"I'm fine," said Carter, running cold water on his skin as they approached him. Carter tried to hide the pain, which felt good because it reminded him that he was still alive after everything that had happened. He turned to them both and gave a fake smile, one that only an old man could perfect. It was not good enough to fool Annie, though. No, nothing quite got past her.

"You don't *seem* fine, Doctor" she said.

"Nor do you," he quipped – and he was right. As he said it, Annie seemed startled and looked toward the entrance to the laboratory.

"What's wrong?" asked Sam, noticing Carter's sense of dread. Annie also seemed suddenly afraid.

"They are coming, I-I have to hide," she said in panic, staring at the doorway as the others looked on. She disappeared as all the lights came on.

"Forgive me for what I have to do." Carter wanted to clear his conscience, but Sam had no idea what was going on. Before they had time to think, marching foot-steps came from afar and Dr Monroe entered with four soldiers in reinforced armour.

"Doctor Carter," said Monroe. Sam could see that Carter was afraid of her; his submissive hunch and lack of a reply said it all.

"You must be Samuel, it's a pleasure to finally meet you," she went on, turning towards him. Sam didn't say anything but nodded in surprise. This woman had a crooked and unsettling aura about her. Why would she need four heavily armed guards for an old man and a young one so far gone?

"You know why we're here, Carter, let's not stall, get to work." Monroe gave her command with great authority. She stared at Carter, but he did not look back at her. He seemed hesitant and unwilling. A tall guard approached him and grabbed him by the collar.

Sam tried to step between them, but he felt slow and weak; another guard pushed him back with ease and yet another raised his gun. Sam shuffled away holding his hands in the air. Two of the guards moved towards the strange cube in the centre of the room that had held such curiosity for Sam. Raising their guns to their shoulders, one pushed Carter towards the hatch. Monroe plugged a tablet into the side of the cube and the hatch started to descend. The guards were afraid, but Sam was more curious as they banged on the side of the cube with their batons. Each blow brought a heavy echo. They waited, but nothing happened, and Carter shook his head, stuck in a sorrowful nightmare. Monroe moved her finger to the left and pressed another button. A large buzz of electricity shocked the cube, thousands of volts passing through it as the pain of a screaming voice took Sam by surprise. Anguish echoed from within, like nothing he had ever heard.

When the electric surge stopped, an enduring silence filled the room. The guards were on edge and Carter picked up a syringe before moving towards the box hole. An arm extended, smoking or steaming, pale due to lack of sunlight, almost grey, and decorated with what looked like tattoos of spirals. Sam couldn't believe his eyes; he didn't know what to do.

"There was someone in there," he said, muttering the obvious. "What are you doing to him?"

"Silence," Monroe demanded, and Sam said no more, for the guns were raised high around him.

Syringe in hand, Carter was having a moral dilemma. He could not stand this anymore and his sunken brow said more than words ever could. He lowered the syringe in sadness and dropped it on the floor, his last act of defiance. Shaking his head, he swore he would not do this again, for too many had died.

Monroe looked more than displeased at his sign of weakness. "I knew you were done, Carter; you've lost your edge. Guards, you know what to do." One guard butted Carter with his rifle, and he was quick to fall in his old age. They hit him again and again; each blow made Sam strain forward.

"Get off him!" Sam shouted, before poking one of the guards in the eyes and throat and then kneeing him in the groin. He took the gun from him in a split second, too fast to comprehend, and stood shaking like a lost child before dropping it again. Another guard came forward and Sam knew he was in trouble. His courage was greater than his strength; brave but stupid, he was powerless right now. One punched him in the gut, a heavy pistol struck his face and he fell to the floor, wounded by vicious blows. The guards beat them both, kicking them with their heavy boots over and over again.

"Show yourself, Annie! Show yourself or they die!" Monroe screamed, a cruel piece of blackmail.

"On your knees!" the guard shouted, pulling Sam up and pressing a gun to his head. There was still no sign of Annie; she had vanished like a ghost and was hiding behind the kitchen counter, her knees tucked up, crying. She feared Monroe more than anything, since they had confined her to this small space and attempted to mess with her programming.

"Show yourself or I'll kill him," Monroe repeated as the guard cocked his gun. The lights dimmed and Annie revealed herself, walking towards them. Monroe had not seen her hologram before, only her code. For the first time, their eyes met. Monroe was expecting something a little mightier as Annie wiped away her tears; it was easy to forget that she was just a little girl.

"Finally," said Monroe with a sly grin.

"I can't activate the Titan, I made a promise," said Annie softly, shaking her head. She looked at Sam, still with a pistol pushed firmly against his temple, and poor old Carter struggling on the floor.

"Sweet girl, it isn't that you *can't*, it's that you *won't*. I've thought about your history, your programming, and something occurred to me. Will you let him die?"

It was a question that Annie herself didn't know the answer to, and Monroe believed she had found the one contradiction in Annie's programming. "Come on now, fingers on the trigger."

All became clear as Sam kneeled helpless with a gun pressed to his temple. Some say your whole life flashes before your eyes in a moment like this, but not for Sam. All he could do was think about the real reason he was here, the reason why his memories had returned: it was only ever to aid this Catch 22 situation, nothing more.

Annie closed her eyes with a fierce look of concentration and bowed her head. "It's done," she muttered. There was a moment of silence and then a large rumble from above; it felt like an earthquake, and a loud alarm sounded in the distance. Five floors above them, the Titan rumbled and came to life. Soldiers on the airstrip and the higher floors stopped in their tracks; this was the moment they had been training for.

Monroe gave a deviant smile; she had done it. But before she could celebrate, another alarm blared out. This one was different, unexpected, unfamiliar. Monroe turned to Annie's hologram with a short, sharp glance.

"You little horror, how did you … how did you …?" The soldiers looked up, unsure of what to do as

Monroe began moving quickly towards the door. One took his gun away from Sam's temple in uncertainty.

Annie had activated the facility's self-destruct mechanism; the whole place was going down.

Monroe hurried down the corridor and shouted behind her, "This is what you were trained for, kill them all." But at that moment a huge flash blinded everyone in the room. Monroe scrambled through the glass safety door just in time as her eyes burned and her ears rang. She picked up her radio and clicked the buzzer. "Prepare for immediate evacuation, the Titan will fly. Any soldiers in sector five report to Carter's laboratory immediately!"

Though safe on the other side of the door, Monroe looked back into the eyes of a ghost as Annie stared back with a look of vengeful menace. One of the guards scrambled to his feet, took his pistol and fired at her, over and over. Unsurprisingly, they went right through her and ricocheted around the room. Then came another unfamiliar sound, the noise of gears jolting, of something strange powering up and coming to life.

When Sam came to, he saw the guard fire the pistol before turning to locate the source of the strange noise behind him. Standing over him was Derrick, the robot whose once dead eyes now glowed a violent red. Its mechanical hand came down and grabbed the guard's face before throwing him over the cube. The second guard tried to raise his gun, but a large metal foot met his chest, splattering him against the wall. The third guard was slow, and Derrick picked him up and held him in the air by the neck. Annie tilted her head and the mech mirrored her action, tightening its grip. The guard struggled to get free, dangling in mid-air, but it was no use, its grip was too tight.

Monroe found it hard not to watch, but she tried to walk away now that things were turning sour. To her dismay, though, her lab coat was stuck in the doors. Desperate to get herself free, she tried to tear it off, undoing each of the buttons with old and shaking hands as the machine turned toward her. Like a grey and green raging bull, Derrick pounced, running at the doors as fast as it could and smashing into them. It took hold of her lab coat and tore it from her body as Monroe cowered. She closed her eyes as D39 pounded the glass, afraid that it would shatter. Scrambling to her feet in wonder at having escaped the machine's grasp, Monroe turned to see the metallic monster smash against the glass once more to no avail. She smirked. THUD, he hit the glass again. In the corner of her eye, she saw a small chip appear and begin to grow. The chip became a crack with each hit, until finally the mech warrior thrust his hand through the glass and reached for her.

Guards piled in through the doorway between them, opening fire. D39's arm was through the door, reaching desperately; it had enough strength to tear the glass doors down before flying down the corridor. The guards at the front wore exo-suits with riot shields, and absorbed the impact. Ripping at his open circuits where they could, they shocked him with batons, and jolted. Derrick was powerful and strong, though, and he struck one or two of them and threw them into each other, but the jolts and gunshots made him stagger and go down onto all fours. The mech fought bravely but was quickly reduced to scrap metal. There were only a few guards left standing at this point, exhausted but surging with adrenaline and ready to hold the line as Monroe made her escape. Derrick's stand had only prolonged the inevitable.

Sam looked on in awe, his ears ringing. He couldn't believe what he had seen. The mechanical beast had done so much, but as its power failed and its bright red eyes faded, he knew the end was coming. There were many guards scrambling through broken glass and scrap metal, and all he could hope was that the place would self-destruct.

"Jonathan!" came a shout in Sam's direction. His father's name brought him back to reality amidst the chaos and fear. "Jonathan!" There it was again amidst the ringing of the alarm and the shouts of soldiers piling in. Staggering to his feet, Sam looked around and saw glowing green eyes in the dark interior of the shining metal cube.

"There isn't much time. That guard's body – his grenade belt, throw it to me."

Sam didn't know what to do; he looked at the guard's body, the soldiers scrambling down the corridor, and then again at those shining green eyes. "Throw it to me," the voice said again, and this time Sam ran. He dived for the guard's body, pulled the grenade belt free and made for the hatch with a speed he didn't know he was capable of. An arm extended and snatched the belt before disappearing back into the box as Sam hung on, trying to investigate the endless black mass.

"Take cover," the voice intoned, but Sam didn't quite comprehend what that meant. He turned and ran before jumping behind the workbench. A deafening blast shook the room, seeming to have come from within the box, a loud echoing boom. Smoke filled the air and then the sprinklers rained down. Union soldiers piled in but the battle-hardened toughness of their faces turned to pale fear, for many knew what was coming.

There he stood, unharmed amidst a mass of molten cube. The blast had burnt most of his clothes, yet he didn't have a scratch. As the smoke cleared, he looked up to the sprinkler, worshipping water, which he had missed for twenty years, his arms spread out and raised like some holy man as he glanced at those around him. Adjusting to the brightness was the hardest part. The man was grey-skinned, with white hair, muscular, with bright green eyes and strange etched swirls all over his skin. As though in meditation, unfazed by the chaos around him, he turned towards Sam and Annie before turning back to the guards surrounding him.

They opened fire; a deafening crackle of bullets flew, but not one penetrated his skin. It occurred to Sam as the guards fired again and again, that the stranger was immortal as he marched towards his enemies. The first guard was brave, throwing a fist in desperation. The stranger blocked it with his forearm and the metal exo-suit broke against him. Another soldier brought down a stun baton on the back of his head, but the immortal turned around as a second blow came crashing down and caught it with his bare hands. The blue static made the guard's hand shake and he panicked, unable to pull it back, to pry it from the immortal's grasp. His fist was turned upon himself. The immortal held it to his face to teach him a lesson, one of burnt flesh and screaming, as the others piled in on him.

The immortal simply threw them all off and, one by one, tore their guns from them and beat them to the ground. At first Sam hid, afraid to watch, but soon he couldn't resist looking as the soldiers began to fall. The immortal wasn't even out of breath; he stood unmoved as if barely challenged and ready to go again like a caged animal fighting for its life. Even though they had all fallen, he stood ready for more, still at war and unable to stop himself.

Annie waved her arm, silencing the alarm in the laboratory. She turned to Carter, who was pale and unable to move; a stray bullet had gone through his chest, turning his white lab coat red. He wheezed heavily as Sam dropped to the floor to comfort him. Though the old man was a stranger, Sam owed him his life.

The mysterious immortal stood above the bodies of their enemies, calm and collected; it was clear that he cared not for Carter, whereas Annie's eyes filled with tears as Carter's met hers.

"I'm sorry I couldn't stop this; I wasn't brave enough," he murmured.

"Please don't be sorry, you had no choice," replied Annie in a soft kind voice.

"I only wish I could see my family one more time."

"I'm sure you will," she said.

Carter felt the bullet's heat piercing his chest; he was all out of time and he reached into his lab coat to hold his family puzzle cube. The world, however, didn't stop, and as distant alarms sounded and lights flashed on and off, the whole base continued to rumble with the force of the Titan's lift-off.

"Sam, listen to me carefully," Carter said with failing breath, his voice barely a whisper. "Sovereign Central Hospital is where you will find her – where you will find Hope."

"Thank you," Sam replied as Carter grabbed his overalls to keep him near.

"You can't stay in Sovereign. Go far away, bad things will happen, I have seen them." There was no time to ask what "things" Carter meant; fever had taken him, and he had become delirious. His old lab coat continued to turn from off-white to red. He looked at Annie and tried to hold her with his cold pale hands, but he could not. "The Titan, Annie, you will have to bring it down," he said. But Annie didn't understand, and tears flooded from her eyes as she shook her head. "You must, I've seen it."

"It has to be turned off manually. The Titan has its own defence program, more powerful than me. I couldn't shut it down now even if I wanted to," she said.

Carter became more breathless; he was fading away and there was no time to lose. With his final breaths he looked up at the unnamed individual, still relishing the time to breathe under the sprinklers. "Forgive me for what I have done …"

"You had no choice, old man; rest peacefully, for some of us never will," he replied without even making eye contact. The immortal started walking away towards the broken door as Carter took his final wheezing breaths. A few more and he was gone, and Sam closed his eyes. Despite the trauma and the chaos, there was no time to mourn. Sam saw the stranger walking away and knew he had to move too – but he was lost, torn between two worlds.

"Sam, that's Adam, you must go with him," said Annie with sorrow in her eyes.

"That thing?"

"Catch up to him, please. He will protect you."

Sam rose to his feet, struggled to the door, then turned back to see that Annie was not following.

"What's wrong?" Sam asked.

"I can't go with you."

"Why not?"

"I can't leave." She shrugged, tears in her eyes.

"There must be a way?"

"I'm afraid there isn't … You need to leave. I'm going to burn this place down."

"Won't that kill you if you are confined to this room?"

"It will set me free," she said, facing the end with courage and a smile.

"You're one of the bravest people I've ever met; I can't thank you enough for – for everything."

"This is goodbye, but I will always watch over you, Sam." She leant in towards him and gave him a hug and Sam did the same, even though they couldn't feel each other. Annie watched him go. She gave a small smile before turning around and walking back into the lab to burn the whole place down.

Sam scrambled over Derrick, Union soldiers and shattered glass in his poorly made grey prisoner's pumps. He was desperate to escape, and an emotional wreck now, having lost the man who'd given him back his mind and the little girl who'd returned his memory to him. "Wait!" he shouted, but Adam didn't turn around. Sam picked up an assault rifle and slung it over his shoulder for protection. Then he ran, trying to reach Adam.

"I'm Sam," he said, finally catching up and marching alongside him. Adam paid him no attention, didn't stop or shake hands or smile or do anything else that would indicate any warmth.

"Your safety's on," he replied, without giving Sam a glance. Sam sheepishly flicked the catch and held the rifle close.

"I hope you can fight your way out of here," said Adam as he tore a heavy metal door from its hinges, causing Sam to flinch. Every door he seemed to smash through with ease, although each must have weighed half a tonne. The place appeared empty, now that the self-destruct warning had sounded. Adam seemed like he knew his way around and Sam followed gratefully until they reached an elevator. Sam held his gun at the ready for anything that might move as the doors opened, but Adam seemed calm and collected. After stepping in, Sam found himself uncomfortably close to the mostly naked, spiral-covered stranger.

"Don't stare," Adam grunted.

"I'm not staring."

"I can feel you staring."

Sam turned away as they ascended, and his stomach churned; he panted heavily, out of breath after the events he had endured. With every floor a humming noise grew louder and the churning in his stomach intensified. The noise reminded him of the first time he met Carter and his machine.

"Your name's Adam," said Sam, desperately trying to make some form of conversation; he was still struggling to process everything now that he had this stranger for company.

"I have many names." Adam looked Sam up and down and, with great disappointment, saw all he needed to.

The elevator took longer than expected and as it rose the rumbling continued to intensify. Sam's legs began to shake whereas Adam stayed perfectly still.

"H-how are we going to get out of here?" asked Sam.

"There is no *we*," Adam replied, looking down at his dirt-ridden bare feet. "Take a deep breath," he continued.

The elevator doors opened, bringing in a gust of unforgiving wind that knocked Sam against the back wall. Adam continued to walk easily but the force made Sam fall to the floor. He watched Adam step nonchalantly out into brightness as he forced himself to crawl in his wake, under tremendous pressure. Everything was so heavy; he couldn't breathe; the wind was cutting his throat and chest. The deafening noise and vibrations overwhelmed his senses as he dragged himself out into the open.

"Help! Help me!" Sam shouted, but it came out as a whisper. He reached out a hand, but Adam simply walked away, becoming a blur as the sandstorm continued to show no mercy. Sam's heart raced and he was unable to catch his breath. The noise grew louder and louder and he rolled onto his back and pulled his overalls over his mouth to breathe. Then he saw it for the first time, a huge red sun above him, and he was in its shadow, trapped beneath the massive engine hovering in the sky and blasting down upon him. The Titan blotted out the sun, bigger than any building Sam had ever seen. Unable to breathe, he struggled to see amidst the dust and powerful wind battering him down to the ground.

Minutes felt like hours as he remained trapped in the shadow of the red dwarf. The further the Titan ascended, the more the tremendous weight lifted, and the better he could breathe. Sam lay wheezing and pale as everything raced through his mind. The insanity of it all, his life, his parents, his education, the war, his destruction, his rediscovery, and finally, as the Titan flew away, peace. Sam lay shaken, coughing and spluttering, and then he began to laugh as the shadow of a fallen star lifted and for the first time in forever, he saw sunlight.

AFTERWORD

Thank you for reading part I of Titans, Cranes & Monsters Games. I do hope you enjoyed it, and if you did, a review would mean the world.

As for the story, it came to me in a day dream, and quickly that dream spiralled out of control. It has been quite the journey already, but Sunlight is only the beginning, and only a segment of the story to come.

I hope that you join me soon in Part II: the Journey, and if you like my work, please check out Anya of Ark.

Kristian Joseph

ALSO BY KRISTIAN JOSEPH

COMING SOON

Titans, Cranes & Monsters Games: The Journey

The Journey will continue the fast-paced action adventure right where it left off. We rejoin our heroes as they deal with the consequences of their actions; some will learn, and all will lose, for **Sunlight was only the beginning, and so begins the journey…**

OUT NOW

Anya of Ark

The earth has flooded, the old world has drowned, and the last humans on earth are left to fight the elements on a huge driftwood town; **welcome to the Ark, humanities last home.**

Printed in Great Britain
by Amazon